LOST™

SIGNS OF LIFE

Don't miss any of the official *Lost* books
from Hyperion!

The Lost Chronicles
Lost: Endangered Species
Lost: Secret Identity

LOST™

SIGNS OF LIFE

FRANK THOMPSON

An Original Novel Based on the Hit TV Series
Created by Jeffrey Lieber and
J.J. Abrams & Damon Lindelof

HYPERION

NEW YORK

ISBN: 0-7868-9092-4

Hyperion books are available for special promo-
tions and premiums. For details contact Michael
Rentas, Assistant Director, Inventory Operations,
Hyperion, 77 West 66th Street, 12th floor, New
York, New York 10023, or call 212-456-0133.

FIRST EDITION

10   9   8   7   6   5   4   3   2   1

For Claire
without whom I'd be truly lost

LOST™

SIGNS OF LIFE

JEFF HADLEY STARED INTO the creature's eyes.

The figure was dark, its features indistinct but disturbing. Malevolent eyes, black pools of hate, glared from its shadowy face. It wasn't moving, but its attitude was threatening, like a snake coiled and ready to attack.

Just behind the monstrous thing, other, similar creatures lurked, half-visible and ominous, quite still but poised to continue their horrible advance. And behind *them* weird, indecipherable symbols floated mysteriously. The signs looked like some strange language, impossible to translate. Jeff thought that if he could only decipher them, they might prove to be clues to an otherwise unsolvable mystery.

Staring at the ghastly things before him, a wave of dread washed over Jeff, bathing him in sweat. Where had these monsters come from? The answer was even more unsettling than the question. He knew that they could only have emerged from one place—from within Jeff himself.

"Dude!"

Jeff whirled around at the sound of the voice, jolted out of what almost felt like a hypnotic trance. Hurley stood behind him, his large frame dominating the space. No one had ever intruded on the tranquil solitude of Jeff's studio before. The dense copse of trees could only be entered by climbing through a narrow passageway between low-hanging, thickly leaved tree limbs. And of all the denizens of the island to have gained entrance, Jeff thought that Hurley was the least likely. He was built along the lines of a refrigerator, not exactly the body type one would expect to be able to easily slither through such a forbidding opening. Whenever Jeff stood near Hurley, he felt a little like Stan Laurel beside Oliver Hardy. In contrast to Hurley's impressive mass, Jeff was positively lithe—tall and thin. Much thinner now, in fact, than normal. His shaggy hair was a coppery red-blond and his beard was so fine, and grew so reluctantly, that even after all this time as a castaway, Jeff's face showed little more than a five o'clock shadow.

Jeff knew Hurley only superficially. Even this, he had to admit, was better than he knew most of his fellow castaways. But even though Jeff could hardly call Hurley a friend, he had always felt comfortable in the young man's presence. There was something about Hurley's wry and affable manner that put others at ease. Jeff, with his Scottish reserve, found the young man's openness and guilelessness to be refreshing—it seemed very American to Jeff. So even though Jeff didn't like being interrupted at his work, he was pleased to see that it was Hurley as opposed to, say, Locke. Jeff didn't like Locke. He didn't trust him.

"Hello, Hurley," Jeff said. "What can I do for you?"

Hurley didn't answer immediately. He seemed to be transfixed by the drawing Jeff had been working on.

Then, snapping out of it, Hurley said, "We're getting together a foraging party for tomorrow. Are you in?"

Damn, Jeff thought. *A day away from the studio. A day of having to deal with the others.* "Sure," he said.

Hurley continued, "Locke says he knows where there's a boar. If he can manage to snare it, it'll take a few of us to haul it back."

"Who else is going?"

Hurley counted on his fingers as he listed the names. "You, me, Locke, Michael—do you know Michael?"

Jeff said, "Kind of." In fact, he didn't know Michael at all. There probably weren't more than half a dozen people on the island whose names had stuck with him.

Hurley continued, ". . . and maybe Sawyer. And that's a big maybe. Sawyer doesn't like to put himself out much."

Jeff shrugged. "Who does?"

Hurley said, "Be nice to have some meat for a change. I get pretty tired of fruit and fish, fish and fruit every freakin' day."

Jeff smiled. "I must admit all that fruit did quite a

number on my digestion for the first week or so we were here. But I'm getting used to it now. Feeling healthier than I've felt in a long time."

"Yeah," Hurley said. "The Island Diet. It's working on everybody but me."

"Oh, come on," Jeff said, "you look like you've dropped at least a stone."

"How much is that in American?"

Jeff did a little mental figuring and then said, "Mmm, it's about fourteen pounds."

Hurley looked dubious, but pleased. As far as he knew, he hadn't lost an ounce since coming to the island, but a compliment is a compliment. "Well," Hurley said, "I do seem to have more energy, I guess."

Jeff said, "What time are we leaving tomorrow?"

"About sunup," Hurley said. "Locke says we've got a lot of ground to cover."

Jeff always preferred to keep to himself and didn't relish the idea of spending a day trekking across the island with the inscrutable Locke. Still, now that he had had a moment to think it over, Jeff admitted to himself that the foraging party sounded like a pretty attractive idea, a jaunt that would do him a world of good. Lately, he had been spending more and more time in the studio— too much, probably. His craving for solitude seemed to be growing day by day. He thought he might be becoming agoraphobic, except that even if you gathered together every single survivor of the plane crash, they still wouldn't make much of a crowd.

But no matter what his self-diagnosis turned out to be, the fact remained that Jeff found comfort and serenity by himself. More than that, he felt protected somehow. But against what? Or whom?

The studio was the perfect sanctuary for a man seeking solitude. The brush was nearly impenetrable on all four sides and many of the trees were seemingly sewn together with vines up top, providing a canopy that was nearly as leak-proof as thatched roofs in Jeff's native Scotland.

Jeff had discovered the little clearing quite by accident. Many of the crash survivors preferred to live on the beach, hoping every day to catch a glimpse of a rescue plane or ship. The rest had moved deeper into the forest, living in caves near a bountiful spring. Jeff saw the latter group as fatalists—those who accepted that they were going to be stranded on this island for a long, long time, perhaps forever. They were settling in; the ones on the beach lived in constant hope. Or fear.

Jeff felt comfortable with neither group. He joined foraging parties to look for food or gather firewood, but he never spoke much to the others, and he went out of his way to keep from forming even the most rudimentary relationships. One day, working at a distance from the rest of a hunting group, he glimpsed an opening in some thick greenery and impulsively crawled through. He was delighted by what he found. In retrospect, he thought it a little odd that his first thought wasn't to use the place as shelter, but as a hideout. Why he should have need for a place to hide away from everyone else was a question Jeff couldn't quite ask himself. But he knew that there was a kind of weird inspiration there. Once inside, he began creating again, for the first time in a long while. He began referring to the place as his studio. And, little by little, it became his home as well. Jeff had been one of the lucky ones who had actually found his own luggage amid the wreckage. The suitcase sat on one side of the studio. On the other was a thick, comfortable pallet of leaves, grass, and straw, over which Jeff had draped a blanket from the plane. Hurley was the first visitor he had ever had here.

Jeff noticed that Hurley was again staring intently at Jeff's latest drawing. "Dude," he said, "that's messed up." He cocked his head, smiled a little, and added, "But it's kind of cool, too. Kind of, um, heavy metal."

Jeff didn't quite know how to respond to this double-edged compliment. "I feel the same way," he said.

Hurley crouched beside him. "Um, you're an artist, right?"

Jeff nodded, a little reluctantly. "Used to be."

Hurley gestured around the space. "Looks to me like you still are," he said. "Look at all this stuff. It's, like, weird. You know? But I like it."

The studio was crowded with sculptures, drawings, peculiar objects made of sticks or clay or fish bones. Some of the works resembled people, but most were abstract: merely shapes that Jeff had found interesting, or textures he had juxtaposed in odd and surprising ways. He spent almost every day at work here, making object after object, drawing after drawing. And virtually no one else on the island had ever seen any of it.

It isn't for them, Jeff thought. *It's for me.*

Hurley said, "You must have some strange stuff going on in your head. Were you a druggie back in the sixties or something?"

Jeff laughed. "I was born in 1970," he said. "So, no."

"Okay, then," Hurley said, "you must have been a druggie in the eighties."

Jeff shook his head. "Wrong again. Never a druggie. Never really a drinker. I've lived a fairly uneventful life." *Ha,* Jeff thought. *There's my first lie of the day.*

"Then where do you get all these out-there ideas?" Hurley asked. He had stood up again and was walking around the studio, studying piece after piece.

Jeff shrugged. He didn't know how to explain to Hurley how different all this was from the art he used to make, the work that had once caused him to be ranked among the most celebrated young artists in Britain. He couldn't talk about how these increasingly disturbing images seemed to emerge full-blown in his imagination, compelling him to create things that almost frightened him. Indeed, there was much that had happened in the last year, before and after the crash of Oceanic Flight 815, that Jeff could not quite put into words. And didn't want to.

Hurley squatted and carefully picked up a small sculpture. There was something vaguely human about it, yet it clearly wasn't meant to be a person.

"What is this?" he asked.

Jeff smiled a little ruefully. "Your guess is as good as mine."

Hurley looked a little puzzled, then nodded. "I saw this show on TV one time about Easter Island," he said. "They've got these awesome stone idols all over the place, and nobody knows who put them there."

Jeff said, "Yes. I've been to Easter Island. When I was in college."

Hurley was impressed. "Cool." He looked closer at the carved rock in his hand. "This kind of reminds me of those things. It's like . . ." He thought hard, trying to come up with the perfect description. "It's like Easter Island on Mars."

Jeff laughed. "Well, I've been to Easter Island," he said, "but never to Mars."

Hurley looked around at the other pieces. When he came back to the drawing that had first caught his attention, he seemed startled. He pointed at the designs behind the mysterious shadow creatures. "What do those things mean?"

Jeff shrugged. "Again, you know as much about it as I do."

Hurley stared harder. "I've seen something just like them."

"On TV?" Jeff asked with a smile.

Hurley shook his head. "No . . ." He rapped his forehead with his fist, trying to shake the memory out of his brain. "No, not on TV. I saw these for real."

2

JEFF HADLEY STARED INTO the model's eyes.

That in itself was testimony to his great professionalism and intense concentration, because the attractive young woman was not wearing a stitch of clothing. When the painting was completed, her body would stand atop a vividly colored mushroom cloud of nuclear holocaust, what Jeff intended as a surrealistic image of sensuality and disaster. He conceived it as kind of a parody of Botticelli's *Birth of Venus,* except that he planned to place the figure within an apocalyptic context. It was typical of the kind of work that was making the thirty-year-old artist something of a phenomenon in the London art world: hyperrealistic, almost photographic renderings of human forms placed in mystical, humorous, or—as in the case of the current painting—horrific settings. Because those human forms were frequently female and naked, Jeff's work had struck a chord with a wider public than had that of some of his peers. But he was also championed by the critics and art dealers, who found the messages embodied in his paintings just vague enough to be endlessly debatable, always worthy of further examination.

Jeff planned his paintings in minute detail. He didn't believe much in inspiration; his art was thoughtful and precise and as perfect as he could make it. To his detractors, the result was a kind of cold soullessness. But to his admirers—and they outnumbered the detractors by a considerable margin—his precision spoke of impeccable technique, of sometimes fantastic ideas brought to vivid life.

All that would come, Jeff knew, with this new painting as well. But, for the moment, it was all about the eyes. The impact of the painting would not depend on the terrifying vision of the ultimate bomb blast or on the erotic lure of the model's body. The meaning would have to be in her eyes. They would have to convey a mixture of seduction and despair.

And Jeff knew he had found the perfect model for the piece. Most models had aspirations to be actresses and, as annoying as that could be, it sometimes made it easier for Jeff to coax them into a specific mood or attitude. Ivy Tennant was no actress, though. She was a struggling twenty-two-year-old art student who occasionally made extra income by modeling for art classes or, somewhat to her shame, posing for nude photographs for Internet porn Web sites.

It was because of one of these Web sites that she had attracted Jeff's attention. He had been giving a lecture at a local university and had noticed her lovely, rather sad face in the class. Afterward, as the students filed out, Jeff heard two boys snickering about Ivy when she walked past. They had stumbled across one of the Web sites and were only too willing to share the address with Jeff when he asked. The next day, after having studied some of Ivy's more explicit photographs, he asked her to model for him. He found her body to be nearly perfect, but she also possessed something that he wanted even more. The seduction and despair Jeff sought were right there in Ivy's eyes—that intriguing mixture seemed to be her natural state.

And, at the moment, there was an added quality of worry in Ivy's eyes.

"Am I doing all right, Mr. Hadley?" she asked softly.

Jeff stopped painting. "Please call me Jeff. And what do you mean?"

She blushed and looked downward. "It's nothing."

Jeff smiled reassuringly. "Please. What is it?"

Ivy said, "Well, usually when I model, the artist or photographer or whoever just can't stop talking about how beautiful I am or what a hot body I have. You know, lech kind of stuff."

Jeff said, "I see."

Ivy looked into his eyes. "But you," she said, "you haven't said a word. And you act like my body isn't even worth looking at."

Jeff was silent for a moment. "Would it make you more comfortable if I talked like the others?"

"Not comfortable, exactly," she said. "It's just . . . I admire you so much. I want to please you."

Jeff pulled a stool closer to Ivy and sat on it. He reached out and took her hand in his. "Ivy, you are one of the most beautiful women I've ever seen. But I chose you for this project for more than your beauty. You have a special quality, something that's yours alone. You deserve better than just to be ogled. You should be treasured."

Ivy shook her head. "I don't like the things they say."

"I wouldn't like it, either," Jeff said. He patted her hand and stood up. "I hope you will be very proud of this painting."

Ivy blushed again. "I'm already proud. Thank you so much."

It would be so easy, Jeff thought. *Like picking a ripe mango from a tree.* He immediately tried to push the thought from his mind. He had had many such dalliances with models. This girl was too fragile. She should be protected, not just used. *Yes,* Jeff thought, *this time I'll do the noble thing.*

Jeff smiled at her and said, "Now let's get back to work."

But there was not much more work done that day. When Jeff stood once again at his easel and looked into Ivy's eyes, they no longer held the haunting quality he sought. Instead they shone bright with pleasure. Nice for her. Bad for the painting.

On their fifth session together, Jeff and Ivy worked late into the night. A prestigious gallery owner was pressuring him to complete the painting and Jeff pushed himself and his model to the point of exhaustion.

Not that she complained. Far from it—the longer the session, the more energized she seemed to be. After nearly a week of working together, Jeff had become keenly aware of a different kind of aura in the room. He had long since completed painting those crucial eyes, and as he devoted session after session to capturing on canvas her luscious body, he sometimes felt his promise to himself slipping away. Sometimes, after staring intently at her for seemingly hours at a time, he would glance up at Ivy's face to find her beaming a slight but knowing smile.

Jeff glanced at his watch. "Oh, my God," he said. "It's nearly two. I'm so sorry."

"That's all right," Ivy said, stretching and yawning. "My first class tomorrow isn't until noon."

"Good," Jeff replied. "You should get to bed."

"I was thinking the same thing." She said it pointedly, gazing deeply into Jeff's eyes.

"Ivy . . ."

She caressed his cheek, then kissed him softly on the lips. "Jeff . . ." she whispered. Ivy smiled wickedly. Now those eyes shone only with seduction.

"It's late," he said. "You should probably get dressed."

She said, "Or not . . ."

And she didn't.

3

"WE GOT FISH!"

The call came from outside, down the beach. Hurley grimaced a little. "Jin comes through again," he said. Then, shaking his head, he added, "I hate fish."

Jeff knew Jin no better than he knew anyone else on the island. He felt a little more justified in this case since Jin spoke no English, only his native Korean. As far as Jeff knew, Jin's wife Sun spoke no English, either. That language barrier made them seem somewhat remote from the other castaways. *But what the hell,* Jeff thought. *I'm pretty remote from the others, too.*

Even though Jeff and Jin weren't pals, exactly, Jeff enjoyed watching Jin at work in the surf. He seemed to have a real knack for bringing in enough fish for everyone, a talent that almost all the others lacked. Locke occasionally brought in a boar and the change in meat was welcome, but Jeff liked fish just fine and thought of Jin as the real unsung hero of the castaways.

Hurley squeezed through the opening of the studio and Jeff followed him outside. A couple of survivors were already gutting the fish and another was stoking the fire. Hurley looked wistful and said, "What I wouldn't give for a steak. Or huevos rancheros."

Jeff smiled. "It's a big island. Maybe there are cows and chickens lurking just over the next ridge."

Hurley didn't seem convinced. He walked over to the cooking fire to lend a hand. Jeff hung back. He was far too preoccupied to be hungry. The drawing he had been working on had unnerved him—something which had been happening more frequently of late—and he welcomed the chance to clear his head a little. He took a deep breath, enjoying the warmth of the sun on his skin and the cool breeze that wafted across the beach. He sat down on the sand and stared out at the vast expanse of ocean before him.

Jeff was always fascinated by how the island was both breathtakingly beautiful and deeply horrifying to him. In many ways he had accepted that this was where he would spend the rest of his life. Others might talk endlessly of rescue or of escape attempts, but deep in his heart of hearts, Jeff knew there was no way out. He felt uncomfortably like a character in one of those devastatingly boring absurdist plays he had willingly sat through when he was a student, when he was at an age to confuse pretentious tedium with depth of thought. Even the better plays in the genre presented an unrelentingly bleak view of humanity. Ionesco. Beckett. None of them offered hope of any kind. Existence is meaningless—grotesque and grim. We waste our lives doing nothing and then we die. And after we die . . . nothing.

But even on days in which such dark thoughts invaded his imagination, Jeff was able to make himself look at the island from an entirely different perspective. Even he had to admit to himself that this place truly was a paradise. There was plenty of food and freshwater. There was always a new place to explore, exciting new things to see and do. Jeff wondered if he had some sort of split personality, compelled to experience the same place both as heaven and as hell.

On the hellish side were some of the odd and unexplained events that had taken place on the island since the crash. Jeff had experienced some of these things himself—the terrible crashing noises, their source unknown, hints that the island was home to some sort of ferocious beast or beasts. And he had seen how the tensions of being castaways had eaten away at the sanity of some of his fellow survivors. Tempers were short; rivalries, even enmities, could erupt from even the slightest conflict.

But Jeff had little to do with the others. Regarding the island monsters that some of the more excitable survivors chattered about, he had seen nothing concrete and he wasn't superstitious. If some sort of creature from a horror film should show its ugly face, he would deal with it then. Sometimes he rather hoped a long-leggedy beastie would go bump in the night, just to break the monotony.

In the meantime, his conscience offered Jeff more than enough disturbing terror for one lifetime.

For his first few weeks on the island, even his conscience didn't haunt him. His mind was too occupied in replaying again and again the horrifying last moments of Oceanic Flight 815.

4

IVY GOT UP MIDMORNING, made herself some coffee, showered, and left for school a little after eleven. Jeff slept through it all.

When Jeff awoke at about one in the afternoon, her scent on the pillow reminded him of the extraordinary early morning hours. He lay back on the pillow with a groan. Jeff was not the type to have a guilty conscience, but at the moment, he felt an unpleasant twinge of remorse. For over a week now, he had told himself repeatedly to stick to business. He could see the vulnerability in Ivy's expressive eyes and knew both that she was his for the asking and that she would see the experience as something far more meaningful than anything he might intend. And because, despite what other faults there were in

Jeff's character, he was essentially a kind man, he did not want to hurt Ivy, but to help her. And so he had instituted a strict hands-off policy.

The truth was that Jeff's experience with Ivy was far from unique. He had been born, it seemed, with two equal talents—creating art and attracting women. Jeff enthusiastically embraced and developed both of his talents, beginning in his early teens, and now his list of romantic conquests was easily as long as his art résumé. In many cases, in fact, the two lists had a great deal in common—many a beautiful woman had ended up both on his canvas and in his bed. *Sometimes,* he thought ruefully, *one of the gallery shows came off like a trip down memory lane, an erotic diary written in oils.*

Jeff comforted himself with the conviction that his serial womanizing was not a crime and, even if so, it was a victimless one. He made no promises of fidelity; there was no talk of forever. He always made it plain—at least it was plain to him—that the encounters were enjoyable, even thrilling, but their life span was finite; a good time had by all, no hard feelings.

Of course, things might go just that way with Ivy. Certainly she had offered herself to *him* and he had given in only reluctantly. Surely she had no expectations, wasn't trying to back him into a serious relationship. *Yes,* Jeff thought with a tentative feeling of relief, *this one is no different from the others. Ships, as they say, passing in the night. But,* he felt with a tremor of dread, *maybe . . .*

His reverie was interrupted by the doorbell. Quickly jumping out of bed and throwing on a robe, he walked over to the door and opened it.

A man in the gray uniform of a London delivery service stood there with a large manila envelope in his hand. When Jeff opened the door, the man squinted at the address label.

"Mr. Jeffrey Hadley?" he asked. Jeff could detect a trace of Cockney in his accent.

"That's right," Jeff said.

The deliveryman pushed a receipt book at Jeff. "Special delivery," he said. "Please sign on line nine."

Jeff signed, then accepted the envelope.

"You any relation to that singer Hadley?" the deliveryman asked.

"Singer?" Jeff asked. "No, I think I've rather lost touch with popular music."

The deliveryman looked deeply offended. "He isn't a pop music singer—he's an operatic tenor, he is."

Jeff smiled apologetically. "Sorry, I don't think so. I've never heard of a singer named Hadley."

The deliveryman looked at Jeff as if he were more to be pitied than censured. "Well, there is one," he said.

Jeff nodded politely, waiting for a follow-up, but the deliveryman wheeled around without another word and walked back down the hallway toward the stairs.

When he saw the return address, Jeff felt a surge of anticipation. It was from the Robert Burns College of Lochheath, Scotland. He opened the envelope with excitement. The letter read:

To Mr. Jeffrey Hadley, Esq.

Dear Mr. Hadley,

It is with great pleasure that the Board of Regents of Robert Burns College of Lochheath extend this offer to you to serve as the school's artist-in-residence, to begin on August 15, 2002.

This position has been filled only rarely over the one-hundred-and-sixteen-year history of Burns College, and is offered only to individuals whose work, teaching skills, and character are of the highest calibre. The board have voted unanimously in your favor and we will feel ourselves honored and proud to count you among our faculty.

Upon your acceptance, you will be contacted by the college bursar for information regarding your lodging, salary, and other particulars.

We do look forward to a favorable response as soon as possible and eagerly anticipate your arrival at Robert Burns College.

Most sincerely yours,

Arthur Pelham Winstead

President, Robert Burns College

Jeff nearly started dancing around the apartment. He had first been contacted by the college nearly six months earlier and had talked with various faculty members on numerous occasions since. They were always careful not to actually offer him the post of artist-in-residence, but it was clear to him early on that it was his if he wanted it. At first, he had been disinclined to take it. Lochheath was just north of Glasgow and was in a surprisingly remote area for such a prestigious educational institution.

But the more he thought about it, the more Jeff began to think that it was the perfect next step. He was just about to turn thirty-two and his paintings generally sold as fast as he could churn them out. But he knew that a wise man had to look to the future. He was realistic enough to realize that, while he might be an enduringly popular artist for the rest of his life, he might also be the flavor of the month. The position at Burns would give him both a steady income and plenty of free time to continue to paint. And perhaps it would even offer him a future he could count upon.

Besides, he had to admit that he got a real charge out of teaching. What were students, after all, but blank canvases on which he could paint colorful layers of knowledge, of curiosity, of promise?

He would regret leaving London, but Scotland was not so far away that he couldn't come in for a bit of excitement now and then. And both Glasgow and Edinburgh were relatively close by. Neither of those cities was London, not by any means, but at least they would offer a taste of the urban experience when the solitude of the remote highlands grew too heavy upon him.

There was one other matter of reluctance. Lochheath was also near the island of Arran, where Jeff had been born. Arran was bleak and forbidding—adjectives that could describe his childhood as well. As soon as he could make a break for it, he had. Jeff left Arran when he was barely sixteen and never looked back. But when he was ensconced on the faculty at Burns College, Arran would be virtually in the neighborhood.

At about four-thirty, another knock came on the door. Jeff was putting the finishing touches on his painting of Venus of the Apocalypse and he walked to the door with brush and palette in hand. Ivy stood there, a large paper bag in her arms. Jeff was a little annoyed at being interrupted, and Ivy sensed it immediately. She smiled nervously.

"I thought . . ." she said timidly. "I thought I'd cook you dinner. . . ." She looked down at the floor as if she expected to be shouted at, or hit. *God,* Jeff thought, *what has her life been like?*

He smiled warmly and stood aside, inviting her to come in. "A great model *and* a great cook?" he said heartily. "You are certainly the rarest and most precious of jewels."

Ivy smiled with relief. She set the bag down on the counter and began extracting groceries and wine. "I'm certainly not a great cook," she said. "But I make a rather wonderful spaghetti sauce, if I do say so myself."

"Then go to it," Jeff said. "Let me finish up here and I'll come make a salad."

Ivy said, "That would be lovely. I'll open the wine."

Ivy's spaghetti sauce was indeed wonderful, or perhaps because they were well into the second bottle of Merlot when they began to eat, it merely seemed so. Jeff lit candles and set the table with the charming ancient china he had inherited from his grandmother. They laughed, ate, drank wine, and made small talk. And then they moved into Jeff's bedroom and made love. It was, at least to that point, the perfect evening.

Afterward, they lay in bed, breathless from exertion. Jeff sat up a little, his arm around Ivy. She rested her head on his chest.

"I'm glad you came over," Jeff said.

Ivy smiled and replied, "I'm glad you're glad."

"Your presence makes this even more of a celebration."

Ivy raised her head and looked into Jeff's eyes. "Is it your birthday?"

"Oh, no," Jeff said. "I've just had some rather spectacular news. You know, of course, what a brilliant and learned lecturer I am."

Ivy nodded with mock solemnity. "Oh, yes, I remember every moment of your lecture last week," she said. Then she grinned. "But I was so busy drinking you in that I'm afraid that I didn't hear a word you said."

"It's a good thing I wasn't grading the class," he said. "I'd have to fail you."

Ivy snickered. "Even when I'm willing to work for extra credit?"

They both laughed and she settled back down onto his chest. Jeff was encouraged. This was going to be easier than he thought.

Ivy said, "So why are we celebrating? Are you giving another lecture at the university?"

"Not exactly," Jeff replied. "Something quite wonderful has happened. I've been offered a place as artist-in-residence at Robert Burns College."

Ivy sat up. "Where is that?"

"It's in Scotland," Jeff said. "In Lochheath, on the shore just north of Glasgow. Burns College isn't a hugely influential school, but the position is a great honor. It makes one feel as though one has really arrived, you know?"

Ivy brought her knees up and wrapped her arms tightly around them. She looked straight ahead. "How long will you be gone?"

Jeff shrugged. "It's hard to say. I'll be there for the year, at least. And I've been given to understand that, under certain circumstances, the position is offered permanently. Not that I'd want to stay for a very long—"

He stopped talking when Ivy's body began quaking with sobs. He was surprised and flustered by the outburst and tried to pull her to him. "Oh, my dear . . ." he said.

Ivy pulled away sharply from his embrace. She continued to weep inconsolably for several minutes as Jeff looked on helplessly. When she finally began to stop crying, Jeff asked, "What's wrong? What have I said?"

She looked at him. Her eyes were red and puffy and her cheeks still wet with tears. "Nothing," she said. "You've said nothing. I was an idiot to have thought . . ."

"Thought what?" Jeff said.

She got out of bed and began pulling on her clothes. She said nothing until she was completely dressed. She picked up her bag and walked toward the door.

"Ivy . . ." Jeff said.

She turned and looked at him with deep sadness in her eyes. "I was an idiot to have thought you were different from the rest."

He stood up and reached for his robe. "But surely . . ." he began.

"Surely I knew I was just a one-night stand," she said bitterly. "Or, to be technical, a two-night stand."

Jeff said, "I'd rather do anything than hurt you."

Ivy opened the door. "Anything? I believe you're exaggerating, Jeff. You have hurt me. You've hurt me more than anyone else ever has. I respected you so much. I was so honored . . ."

She walked out and closed the door quietly behind her. For a moment, Jeff considered running after her. But for what? Even if he could make her feel better now, it would only delay the inevitable. *Better to end it quickly,* he told himself. *She'll feel better tomorrow.*

He had told himself something similar on many occasions. Now he wondered if it had ever been true. Jeff sat down on the edge of the bed. *I am,* he thought to himself, *a terrible person. A terrible, terrible person.*

5

SITTING ON THE BEACH, Jeff had plenty of time to re-member and reflect upon the way he had treated Ivy. He would have considered it one of the low points of his life if it hadn't turned out that he would quite soon after treat someone else far worse, and pay a far greater price for it.

In many ways, all that seemed so far away now— London and Scotland and the women whose lives he had touched, and who had touched his. All those things were distant in a sense greater than geography; they almost seemed like places, beings, and happenings from a com-pletely different world. Now Jeff's entire existence con-sisted only of this island and the people who had survived with him. There was no escape from either and so, as far as Jeff was concerned, this place was its own planet; he had rocketed there like a space traveler from Planet Past.

Actually, he thought with grim humor, *a rocket would have been far safer than the conveyance that really* did *bring us here.* He thought back on that day with the most banal of laments: *Had I but known . . .*

No one ever boards an airplane without experiencing even a subliminal frisson of fear that the plane is going to crash. Most people suppress the thought quickly; the tedium and discomfort of flight takes the mind to other places. But even though everyone fears it, most passengers don't truly believe that they are boarding a machine that will kill them in a few hours or minutes. It is an abstract fear, one that is, we tell ourselves, only in our minds.

And so it was with Jeff Hadley that day. He was not a particularly religious man, but he always uttered a quick and quiet prayer as the plane began its ascent. After he had made his peace with a merciful God, he closed his eyes, hoping to make the talkative tourists seated on either side of him believe that he was asleep. It worked so well that soon he *was* asleep. And when the screams of terrified passengers and the ear-cracking roar of tearing metal jolted him awake, he viewed the scene of chaos with a strange kind of detachment. He hadn't *really* believed he was going to die, despite the content of his prayer. And now, even when the prospect seemed ever more likely, Jeff remained surprisingly calm and distant, almost bemused. *So this is how I go out,* he thought. *Not how I would've guessed.* Crazily, he found himself listening to an almost mocking voice in his head, singsonging, *Oh well, we all gotta go sometime!*

Jeff had never believed all that guff about out-of-body experiences, but he realized that he was experiencing something like that now. He felt almost as if he were seated in a different part of the plane, serenely watching a film about his own impending doom. His life didn't flash before his eyes, and he was slightly disappointed to realize that this cherished cliché probably wasn't going to come true in his case. The only thing that flashed before his eyes was his death; or, at least, what he assumed would soon be his death. The tourist to his right, an overweight man in a loud orange shirt and unbecoming Bermuda shorts, unbuckled his seat belt for some reason and tried to run down the aisle. When the back of the plane broke away and row after row of screaming passengers was sucked out into the abyss, the brightly hued tourist followed them headfirst. He held his hands out before him and he looked to Jeff a little like Superman as played by Buddha.

A young Asian woman in the row in front of him twisted around at the noise of the split and for a moment her terrified eyes met Jeff's. He wanted to smile at her and he tried to think of something comforting to say. But when he opened his mouth, Jeff was rather surprised to find that, instead of speaking, he was actually screaming at the top of his lungs.

Later, Jeff hoped that he would find the young woman among the survivors, to make sure that she had come through the ordeal all right. But even though he often felt a momentary thrill when he caught sight of Sun, he always immediately realized with a sinking heart that it wasn't the same woman. Jeff guessed sadly that she and her terrified eyes had followed the portly Superman.

The young woman's face was the last sight Jeff remembered seeing in the air. He'd grabbed at the oxygen mask that had dropped before his face but could never remember if he had actually put it on. At first he thought all the air had been sucked out of the cabin, because suddenly he couldn't breathe. He jerked his head upward and inhaled with a deep gasp and only then realized that he had been lying facedown in a shallow tide pool. He sat upright, dimly trying to work out how he had gotten from a seat in the economy class section of an airliner to this little pool of seawater.

Jeff gingerly flexed his arms and legs and found everything to be in working order. He felt warm liquid on his face, wiped it, and came away with a bloody hand. He had several small cuts and scratches on his forehead and cheek and a fairly nasty slash across his chin, but nothing too serious, at least as far as he could tell.

An intense young man with close-cropped hair and a disheveled business suit came sprinting over to Jeff.

"Are you all right?" the man asked.

Jeff nodded. "I think so."

The young man peered at the cuts on Jeff's face. "I don't think any of those are real bad. Clean the wounds with seawater and try to get a bandage around that chin."

Jeff nodded again and started to rip the sleeve from his shirt. The young man said, "Good. And when you're ready, come help. There's a lot of people in worse shape than you."

"I will," Jeff said. Using the torn-off sleeve as a washcloth, he sat in the tide pool and cleaned his minor wounds. The chin kept bleeding freely, so he pressed the cloth hard against the cut for a few moments. Then he rinsed the blood from the sleeve and wrapped it around his face, just under his mouth. He tied it at the back of his head.

My God, he thought. *I must look like a bandit whose mask has slipped off.*

For Jeff, the rest of that terrible day was a blur of activity—helping to rescue luggage and provisions from the broken body of the plane, giving whatever aid he could to other hurt passengers, trying to convince himself that he had not slipped into some nightmare from which he could never awake.

That first night, Jeff was too exhausted even to try to seek shelter. The weather was cool and the night sky clear and shimmering. He lay down on the sand just out of the reach of high tide, and immediately fell into a deep and dreamless sleep.

In the days and weeks that followed, Jeff worked alongside the others but said little. His mind seemed to have completely emptied itself. He gathered food and firewood and helped build rudimentary shelters for himself and others almost as if he were a robot, programmed to complete necessary tasks. He learned a little about his fellow survivors. The young man who had looked at Jeff's cut face on the first day was named Jack. For reasons that Jeff never really understood, Jack emerged as the de facto leader of the castaways. He seemed to inspire respect and loyalty among the others—at least, most of the others. There was a rough, rather ill-tempered man named Sawyer who had a contentious relationship with Jack and sometimes, it seemed to Jeff, the two of them were on the verge of attacking each other.

This kind of drama would have been of interest to Jack back in Scotland, but somehow here it meant little. Others doubtless knew why Sawyer and Jack appeared to hate each other, but Jeff just didn't care. In fact, he didn't seem to care about anything.

As Jeff continued to gaze out at the gentle sea, he almost missed the blankness of those early days. He supposed he had been in shock, that merciful state that shuts down the mind and emotions when they can't handle an overload of stress or horror. And as he emerged from that shock, he found himself once again facing some of the truly terrible things that had been hiding in his head. And that was when the dreams started.

The dreams were at first merely vague—menacing, half-seen figures, odd shapes. Everyone seemed to speak in a language that Jeff didn't understand . . . and yet he did. When he awoke he was puzzled by what he had seen in the dreamscape, but could only remember flashes of imagery. And when he impulsively began sketching those weird symbols, he didn't connect them with the dreams at all. Even after he started making things, drawing pictures every day, he never wondered where his inspiration was coming from. On some level, he was glad to be creating again, even if this new art bore no resemblance to anything he had ever done before. Jeff didn't think much about that difference, either; he just kept working. If it ever did occur to him, even in passing, that he was traveling in an entirely unfamiliar artistic direction, he dismissed it immediately as being the natural result of working under vastly different circumstances with only those tools he could scrounge up from the island.

But today Hurley's presence had forced Jeff to look at his island art for the first time. Jeff thought hard about the latest drawing he had been working on and was almost startled by it, as if he were only now fully aware of what he had sketched onto the lined notepaper. Not for the first time, he had the odd feeling that he created this artwork directly from his unconscious. Even more oddly, it almost felt as if it were created by someone else, with Jeff merely the instrument. Jeff could almost take comfort from that fact because, especially recently, he had been unleashing nightmarish visions that he had no desire to claim as his own. What was at first merely eccentric attempts at "found" art had begun to metamorphose into darker, more disturbing imagery. The malevolent creatures in the drawing Hurley found so disturbing had been creeping into Jeff's work with greater clarity and frequency.

Looking out at the sea, Jeff thought about how out of place these visions of horror seemed to be in such a lush and gorgeous setting. Down the beach, several castaways sat or squatted in a semicircle around the cooking fire, eating the fish Jin had caught. Hurley was nowhere to be seen.

The tide was coming in, and each wave lapped closer and closer to the place where Jeff sat. But he was too deep in thought to notice. Something that Hurley had said only a little while ago kept replaying in his mind. As they stood together in Jeff's studio, Hurley asked the standard question that all artists, sooner or later, are asked:

"Hey, dude," Hurley said, "where do you get your ideas?"

Jeff shook his head. "I'd tell you if I could," he said. "But these things just come to me. I just wake up in the morning and . . ." He waved his hand at all the pieces that lined the grassy floor of the studio.

Hurley nodded thoughtfully. "You must dream it all."

"Perhaps," Jeff said.

"You know what you ought to do?" Hurley said. "You ought to keep one of those, what do you call 'em . . . ? Oh, yeah, dream journals."

The statement startled Jeff. Savannah used to tell him the same thing.

6

WHEN JEFF HADLEY ARRIVED at Robert Burns College in Lochheath, Scotland, he felt like a real celebrity. True, his reputation had been growing quickly in London and he was used to being feted by gallery owners, acclaimed by critics, and courted by art collectors eager to latch on to the next big thing. But London was too big, and the pool of celebrity too vast for Jeff ever to feel like a true star.

But from the moment he stepped off the train in Lochheath, he knew that things were different. There was a welcoming committee on the platform, and one middle-aged woman, Jeff was amused to note, actually held a large sign reading WELCOME JEFF HADLEY! He stepped off the train, a suitcase in his right hand and a tweed overcoat draped over his left arm. When the cheer of welcome went up, he paused on the top step, feeling as if he were reliving a moment from an old film. Actually, he had chosen to make the journey by train instead of driving up just so he could make such an arrival. But he didn't really expect anyone to play along. And when he looked out on the small sea of some forty beaming faces, he was both delighted and slightly embarrassed.

A tall man of about fifty stepped forward, holding his hand out to Jeff. He had thick black hair, close-cropped, and was dressed neatly in a three-piece suit. Jeff recognized him from their previous meetings and remembered him as being something of a nerd. Still, he told himself, he was immersing himself in academia now and knew that if he held a prejudice against nerds, he would be a lonely man indeed.

"Mr. Hadley, Mr. Hadley, Mr. Hadley," the man said with syrupy enthusiasm. "I am Gary Blond. Delighted to see you. Simply delighted!"

Jeff shook his outstretched hand, smiled, and said, "Of course, Mr. Blond. I remember you well. How nice to see you again." Mr. Blond beamed with pleasure at being remembered by so august a personality and turned to the little crowd. "Fellow faculty members," he said loudly, "please welcome our prestigious new artist-in-residence, Mr. Richard Hadley!"

Everyone applauded wildly. Jeff bowed slightly and smiled as warmly as possible. "Thank you very much," he said. "Er, but one small correction. My name is Jeffrey Hadley, not Richard—but I hope you will all call me Jeff."

Mr. Blond laughed in a high-pitched shriek at his faux

pas. He slapped himself good-naturedly on the forehead and said, "Blond by name, blond by nature!" No one else laughed, evidently not amused by the man's asininity, but Jeff kept the wide smile on his face to indicate to one and all that he was neither embarrassed nor offended. He hoped he gave off the aura that he was just a regular chap and not some ivory-tower artist who was unapproachable by the regular folk.

The rest of the day was an exhausting swirl of introductions, two receptions—one with tea and sandwiches, one with an open bar—and finally a dinner with most of the other art instructors and professors. With the exception of Mr. Blond, the other faculty members struck Jeff as pleasant and intelligent people. The college president, the grandly named Arthur Pelham Winstead, was away at an academic conference. Jeff was relieved to hear it—just one fewer person to meet and engage in bland small talk.

But Jeff did notice that more than a few of the female staff members were quite attractive. He carefully filed that little fact away with a certain degree of caution.

Steady on, Jeff said to himself. *Remember we're turning over a new leaf. That way lies trouble.*

At the end of the long, long day, Mr. Blond drove Jeff to his new home. Even by the dim illumination of the single streetlight before it, the cottage was picturesque and inviting, evocative of every Scottish cliché of charm. The walls were of gray stone. The front door was trimmed with wide slabs of limestone, as were the two large windows that flanked it. Two gables jutted out from the slate roof on the second floor. In between them was a small skylight—obviously a modern addition to an ancient house.

Mr. Blond carried in Jeff's suitcase and set it down in the foyer. Jeff followed him in and stood at the entrance, taking stock of the first floor. To the left was a sitting room. Someone had come ahead and started a lively fire in the fireplace. To the right was a small dining room. Three candles blazed from a brass candelabrum on a lace tablecloth.

Directly ahead of Jeff were stairs rudely carved from thick slabs of wood. Mr. Blond pointed at the steps and said, "The kitchen is yon, just behind the staircase. And up here . . ." he began walking up the stairs ". . . is your bedroom."

Jeff walked up behind him, careful not to get punched in the nose with his suitcase, which Mr. Blond was swinging rather wildly. At the top of the stairs, the bedroom was large but with a low ceiling. The odd proportions of width without much height reminded Jeff of the home he had lived in during his childhood in Arran. The bed was large, with an overstuffed mattress, four huge pillows, and a thick, luxurious comforter. The fireplace here, too, was merrily ablaze. Jeff thought that the whole thing looked like a cinema art director had created it for a fairly unimaginative film set in Scotland. And again, as at the train station, he was both touched and amused.

Mr. Blond looked around in satisfaction. "The decorating committee have done a splendid job, eh?" he said.

"Yes, indeed," Jeff said, eager for Mr. Blond to go away. "And that bed looks particularly inviting, after such an arduous day." Then he added, so as not to offend Mr. Blond, "Arduous, but pleasant."

"Indeed," Mr. Blond replied. He set Jeff's suitcase on a stand near the tall oak wardrobe. Then he just stood there, smiling pleasantly at Jeff.

"Well, um . . ." Jeff said. "As I said, the bed looks *most* inviting."

Mr. Blond looked surprised. "Oh," he said. "You want to go to bed *now*. Well then, let me push off and leave you to it."

Jeff shook Mr. Blond's hand and said, "Thank you for everything."

"Oh, tut tut tut," said Mr. Blond. "We are so pleased and honored to have you here."

"Oh, the honor is all mine," Jeff said, feeling that this cross-talk act was going to go on all night, "and I'll see you first thing in the morning."

"Yes yes yes," said Mr. Blond. Jeff was growing quite weary of the man's habit of stating everything in triplicate. "First thing. Indeed indeed indeed."

When Mr. Blond finally walked out the front door and Jeff heard the car start, he breathed a sigh of relief. Now that the house was Blondless, he could take in its considerable charms with more appreciation. He walked into the small, low-ceilinged living room and sat down in a large overstuffed chair that had been placed near the fire. There was a small table beside it on which stood a bottle of brandy and a single snifter. He poured himself a healthy dose and sipped it appreciatively. Soon, with the combined effects of the fire and the brandy, he was nicely warmed both inside and out. And the chair was so very comfortable that, despite how inviting the bed upstairs had looked, Jeff found himself blinking back sleep for a few seconds and then was out.

He awoke when the sun's rays shone through the window shade and directly into his eyes. He stood up with an unaccustomed stiffness and realized that he had probably not moved a muscle all night long. He walked back into the kitchen and began opening cabinets. He found that someone—perhaps the decorating committee of which Mr. Blond was so proud—had done some grocery shopping in anticipation of Jeff's arrival. He found tea, coffee, eggs, bread, butter, sugar, and orange juice. Only coffee sounded appetizing at the moment, and he soon had a pot started.

He sipped the coffee in a sturdy wooden chair set on the steps outside the back door. Jeff's back garden was small but lushly green. It would be comfortably shady in the summer and even on this brisk autumn morning he already knew that he had found his favorite spot in his new home.

Jeff was immediately comfortable and happy at Robert Burns College. Lochheath was typical of many of the hamlets that dot the Scottish countryside. Rows of stone houses and small businesses, the buildings often joined in groups of three or four, lined both sides of a wide street. There were four parish churches, and their steeples rose above the thatched or slate roofs, offering the traveler either literal or spiritual direction, whichever his need.

Just beyond Lochheath, a dark sea crashed fiercely onto a rocky shore. Brave fishermen in flimsy-looking boats set out each day in search of a bounteous catch. They and their forebears had forged an uneasy alliance with the angry ocean for centuries. Jeff loved both the sight and the sound of the sea. Even in his cottage, nearly three miles from the beach, he could sometimes hear its powerful roar and he felt comforted.

His celebrity had, of course, preceded him and from the beginning his lectures were packed. He was gratified to learn that many of the students possessed true talent and he soon had a vibrant, if unofficial, master class going on in the large studio attached to his office.

The eagerness of his students to ingratiate themselves with the great painter often offered Jeff other kinds of temptation, as one enthusiastic and nubile college girl after another made it known to him that they themselves had lessons to teach him. Jeff's inner mind urged him to take each young woman's offer seriously, but his greater conscience stubbornly resisted the easy pickings.

Of course, this did not mean that Jeff had turned into a monk as well as a professor. To the contrary, the field of available gallery owners, museum workers, and art critics, not only in Lochheath but in Glasgow, proved to be nearly inexhaustible. And, once every three or four months, Jeff returned for a long weekend to London, where his pool of contacts was still considerable. He often told himself that if he spent even half the energy on his art as he did on the art of seduction, he might yet turn into a painter of true greatness. But, he then had to admit, the trade just didn't seem to be a fair one.

Because Jeff's romantic life was filled with great variety—if not much true emotion—he was able to erect an impenetrable mental barrier between himself and even the most comely of his female students.

But that barrier fell with a crash the day he met Savannah.

Jeff was forever after a little puzzled why Savannah McCulloch made such a powerful impact upon him. Looked at dispassionately, she was no more beautiful or sensual than any of a dozen other young women in his class. She was a talented artist, but was by no means a prodigy or a genius in the making. She was intelligent and had a quick sense of humor, but the same could be said of many others. Nevertheless, from the moment he saw her in the second row of his lecture, sketching earnestly in an oversized pad of drawing paper, he was smitten in a more powerful way than he could ever remember.

At five feet ten inches, Savannah was taller than most of the other girls in the class. Her hair was long, reaching nearly down to her waist, and the color of sand. Sometimes she wore it in a long thick braid but when it flowed freely, Jeff thought she looked like something out of a Botticelli painting. Her eyes were a pale blue but there was an intensity behind them that made them seem literally to flash, a phenomenon that Jeff had always considered just a literary cliché.

And it was, he decided later, her eyes that had captured him. Just as Ivy's haunted eyes had started the sequence of events that would end in his breaking her heart.

Throughout that first class, at the beginning of Jeff's fourth year as artist-in-residence at Burns College, it seemed to him that Savannah's eyes were boring into his like lasers and he felt so self-conscious under her relentless gaze that he lost track of his lecture more than once.

Afterward, as the rest of the class filed out, Savannah walked up to Jeff's desk.

"I think you're wrong, you know," she said pleasantly.

Jeff was startled. "Excuse me?"

"Your whole obsession with realistic detail," she said. "That was all well and good back in the old days. But photography took care of that. Now art should go to places where realism can't do the job."

Jeff leaned back in his office chair and smiled. "And you are . . . ?"

"Savannah McCulloch," she said. "I'm a painter."

Jeff nodded. "Well, I find your theory quite compelling. So did the Impressionists, oh, more than a century ago."

"Well, you clearly didn't take the message of the Impressionists to heart," she said, smiling. "Now, Jackson Pollock—that's more like it!"

Jeff smiled again. "So you'd find my work more compelling if I simply threw a can of paint at a canvas and let it drip wherever it might instead of painstakingly working out a perfectly executed image?"

"Wouldn't you agree that the search for that kind of perfection just sucks the blood out of the creative process?" she said.

Jeff leaned forward. "How old are you?"

"I am twenty-two years old," she said, "a fact that has absolutely no relevance to this conversation at all."

"Oh, I think it has great relevance," Jeff said. "That's why I've entertained the subject this long."

Savannah narrowed her eyes. "What do you mean?"

"I mean that the very young are entitled to spout stupidity with absolute conviction," he said. "It's only after we grow older and learn much, much more that we realize how little we know."

"Hmm," she said, still pleasantly, "both a commercial whore *and* condescending. Be still, my beating heart!"

"If you find my views and my technique so abhorrent," Jeff said, "I wonder why you have bothered to take my class at all."

Savannah laughed. Jeff was entirely charmed by the sound. She said, "Because I aim to be a commercial whore myself. I just don't have the technique yet!"

Now Jeff was laughing with her. He wasn't completely sure whether she had truly insulted him or if she was just having fun with him. Either way, he realized with a jolt of pleasurable panic, he had just fallen in love.

7

THEY CAME QUIETLY AT first, so quietly that Jeff did not so much hear their approach as feel it. He blinked hard, trying with all of his will to peer into the thick haze that surrounded him. But nothing revealed itself.

Nothing.

Jeff didn't know if he was in a pit or a cave or a locked room or purgatory. All he knew was that he was about to learn something that he very much did not want to know. A dark sheet of dread draped itself over his soul, and his body nearly convulsed with the trembling brought on by the exquisite agony of unbearable suspense.

He looked around desperately. If he could just see where he was, maybe he could figure out what was after him. If only something would show itself. Even a terrible

monster would be better than this awful waiting and wondering. At least then he would know what he had to fight,
or what had come to destroy him. As terrifying as the idea
was, ignorance was even more terrifying.

Then, out of the mists, they almost began to show
themselves. A sweep of fabric here, a deepening shadow
there. Eyes that did not glow but were starkly visible
nonetheless. Jeff covered his face with his hands, but
peeked through his fingers, as he had done when he was a
child watching a horror film.

The things were all around. Not people, not creatures,
just . . . things. Jeff wanted to run screaming, but he had
no idea which way to go. And, astonishingly, as much as
he was impelled to flee, he felt an even stronger urgency
to follow them into the impenetrable mist. He stepped
forward, almost unable to believe his own actions. They
were leading him, he knew now. They had come for him
and were taking him to a place that was prepared for him.
Jeff gasped for air and held his hands before him like a
sleepwalker.

As he stepped cautiously forward, he heard something
that sounded almost like whispering. The deeper into the
fog they stepped, the louder the whispering became. It
sounded almost like speech, but it was no language that
Jeff had ever heard, or even imagined.

Jeff had an indefinable feeling that he had reached
his destination, and stopped walking, although nothing
he could see indicated that he had traveled more than a
few inches. But he could feel that they were showing
him something and when he thought about what they

might want him to see, his trembling redoubled, his body jerking as if he had stuck his tongue into an electrical outlet.

And although the fog did not seem to clear, Jeff somehow began seeing through it. He now felt he was in a dark underground chamber of some kind. Before him, the walls were covered with drawings and carvings. Odd shapes. Strange. And, he realized with a violent start, just like the ones he had been making since he arrived on the island.

The terrifying figures closed in, surrounding him. They pressed in close but were as horribly indistinct at that proximity as they had been from the start. Perhaps they were wearing robes, Jeff thought. Perhaps not. It could be that their bodies were simply flowing and malleable, like cloth.

They were all observing him with their malevolent glares, but one of them seemed to stare directly at him in a most meaningful way, as if trying to communicate something profound. Was it Jeff's imagination, or was this one a woman? A woman with long, light-colored hair and delicate features? How could it be? He couldn't see the others clearly enough to determine even if they were human, much less male or female. But this one was different.

Looking deeply into Jeff's eyes, she held something high over her head. Fearfully glancing upward, Jeff saw that it was a flat circle about a foot in diameter with an intricate design in the middle. He realized that the thing was a talisman of some sort. It seemed to be made of highly polished wood. The female said nothing but continued to hold the object high with both hands, seemingly willing Jeff to understand its meaning.

And then he began to understand. *Yes*, he thought. *Yes, of course. It's the key . . .*

Jeff awoke with a violent shudder. His face was wet with perspiration and he was lying on the floor of the studio several feet from the pallet of leaves and branches he normally slept upon.

He sat upright and held his head in his hands. Already the dream was beginning to drift away. The talisman's meaning had seemed so clear to him, but now that he was awake, all he could remember of the dream was the terror. Oh, and the woman. These nightmares had been coming more and more frequently, but he was pretty sure that the woman had never shown up before. He knew that must mean something, but at the moment all he could do was tremble and try to force himself to relax.

And as he took deep, calming breaths, something else came back to him—the talisman itself. He still couldn't quite remember what he thought about it, but he remembered what it looked like.

He stepped outside. The full moon was high overhead, casting the beach in a soft, white glow. A couple of campfires broke the darkness here and there, but if there were other island dwellers awake at this hour, Jeff didn't see them. He walked over to his junk pile. For weeks, whenever he saw an interesting bone or seashell or chunk of driftwood, he brought it back to the studio and tossed it on the pile. He figured that sooner or later, he would find a use for it in some art project or another. And he knew that there was in the pile the perfect piece for his current inspiration.

After digging around for several minutes, the search made more difficult by the low level of light, he stood upright, holding a large, thick square plank in his hand. Where it had come from, he had no idea. It looked like a wide board that had been cut with a saw. Jeff doubted that it had come from the plane, and doubted that there had ever been a saw on this island. But no matter—that was a mystery that could be pondered another day.

For the moment, he had to get to work. He sat down beside the entrance of the studio and leaned back against one of the thick palm trees that formed the walls. And after sharpening his pocketknife on a stone, he began to carve a talisman.

8

JEFF CARVED THE PIECE through the night. The need for sleep finally caught up with him just as the dim light of dawn began spreading subtly across the beach. He felt as if he had slept for slightly under a millisecond when he was roughly shaken by the shoulder.

"Rise and shine," Hurley said, leaning over Jeff. "Time to go bag us a boar."

Jeff groaned. He was still leaning up against the tree. He had been sitting with crossed legs on the sand and now both knees creaked and ached as he gingerly straightened out and prepared to try to stand.

"Oh, God," he said. "Surely the boar will be just as tasty if we catch it later this afternoon."

Hurley shrugged. "Locke says the morning is best. Maybe the boar likes to sleep in, too."

Hurley offered a hand. Jeff took it and struggled to stand upright. *I feel like I'm seventy years old,* he thought.

"Well, I know how the boar feels," Jeff said. "In fact, at the moment, I know how the boar will feel when Locke gets hold of him."

Hurley nodded solemnly. "It would be great to have some coffee, wouldn't it?"

"Indeed it would," Jeff said. "Indeed it would."

A small group of boar hunters had gathered down near the spot where the fish had been cooked the night before. Some of the coals still glowed red and the sand was littered with fish bones.

Jeff recognized most of the men in the group. Locke was tall and straight with steely eyes and a head that he kept shaved. Jeff figured he must have been a military man; Locke reminded him of those hard, indomitable men from the adventure stories he read as a boy—the kind of man who would join the French Foreign Legion or live in the jungle on swamp water and live rats. Locke frightened Jeff a little, although their few meetings had always been blandly pleasant.

Beside Locke stood Michael. As with Locke, Jeff had only encountered Michael occasionally, but he instinctively liked him for no more apparent reason than he disliked Locke. Michael's eyes were kind, and Jeff had observed the obvious affection between Michael and his son, Walt. And now that Hurley had told Jeff that Michael was an artist, he was eager to talk shop with him. The very thought surprised him a little. He hadn't been eager to talk to anybody about anything since they had first crash-landed here in this verdant purgatory.

Charlie was also there. His sleepy face broke into a grin when he spotted Hurley and Jeff approaching, and he waved a greeting. Locke and Michael were packing shoulder bags with bottles of water and pieces of fruit. When Locke noticed the new arrivals, he stood up and tossed them each a travel pack. Jeff noted that Sawyer was not among those present, nor was Dr. Jack. He wondered if the two antagonists simply avoided each other, or if both merely had more important tasks here at camp today.

"Morning," Locke said, smiling. It was a perfectly friendly smile, Jeff thought, so why did it chill him so?

"Morning is right," Hurley said. "Personally, I can think of at least one place I'd rather be than here."

Michael laughed. "I heard that!" he said. "I was dead to the world when this one"—he jerked a thumb at Locke—"came interrupting my beauty sleep." Michael looked at Jeff and held his hand out. "You're Jeff, right? Glad you're coming along."

Jeff shook Michael's hand and then gave a general greeting to everyone. He had the silly feeling that he was the new kid in school, the outsider among the popular kids. Charlie also shook Jeff's hand and said, "You're the one who found a natural-grown house, right?"

Jeff nodded. "I guess so," he said. "Just a stroke of luck."

Locke smiled that icy smile again. "No such thing as

luck," he said. He walked over to a lean-to on which were propped several spears; actually, they were simply reasonably straight branches or bamboo stalks with sharp points which had been carved by Locke.

"Some of you guys have never gone boar hunting," he said. "It can be dangerous, so I want everybody to stick together and take no chances. I'd much rather come home without a boar than to come home without one of you."

"Or you," said Michael, his eyes twinkling.

Locke didn't smile back. "Not likely," he said. "We'll all have spears. I also have this." He pulled a large knife with a long serrated blade from the sheath on his belt. "The spears will bring down the boar—we hope—and, if we can get him down, then I can finish him off. Probably that'll be the easy part. Lugging several hundred pounds of ham and bacon back to the camp will be where the hard work comes in."

No one said anything. Jeff found himself unexpectedly excited by the prospect of the hunt. Back in England, he would have found the idea appalling. Indeed, he probably would have joined a picket line, marching against it. Maybe, he thought, he was turning into Elemental Man; maybe they would all eventually regress to the state of savages. After all, he'd read *Lord of the Flies*. He knew what could happen; what probably *would* happen.

Locke handed a spear to each man. "If you can carry two of 'em, that probably wouldn't be a bad idea," he said. "There's no telling what we'll need before this is over."

Charlie asked, "How far do you think we'll have to travel?"

Locke pointed to a peak in the distance. It looked to Jeff to be about five miles away. "The last time I harvested a boar, I saw several piglets in that area," he said. "If we're lucky, they haven't strayed too far from home. Maybe there are some adults there, too. Either way, we'll take what we can get."

He gestured to the bags. "We've all got enough water for a day," Locke said. "I hope we'll be back by nightfall. But even if not, there are more springs back in the forest there, so we'll be fine on that front. We should go easy on the fruit, though. Maybe we'll find something on the way, maybe not."

Hurley grinned at Jeff. "Maybe we'll find some of those cows you were talking about."

Jeff laughed.

"What's this?" Locke asked.

"Nothing," said Jeff. "Hurley and I were just talking yesterday about how much we'd enjoy a nice steak."

Locke smiled. "Wouldn't we all?" he said.

"Amen to that!" Michael added.

Locke turned and started walking and the others fell in behind him. As Locke had suggested, each carried two spears. Jeff immediately began using them as walking sticks, holding one in each hand. He thought, absurdly, that he looked as if he were cross-country skiing. The thought flitted across his mind that he would never be able to do that again. Indeed, he would probably never see snow again. But as soon as the depressing and discouraging idea hit, Jeff tried to banish it. Walking just behind Michael, and almost by his side, Jeff said, "Hurley tells me that you're an artist."

Michael nodded. "That's right. He told me the same thing about you."

Jeff laughed and said, "Where was Hurley when I was back in England and needed a press agent? He seems to be able to spread the word pretty effectively."

Up ahead, Hurley twisted around a little and called, "If you're gonna talk about me, you'd better keep it clean!"

Walking just behind Hurley, Charlie smiled wickedly back at Michael and Jeff. "But if you talk about me, make it as dirty as possible! Ah, you never appreciate the groupies when you have them! But you sure miss them when you don't."

Jeff looked questioningly at Michael.

"Charlie used to be in a rock band," Michael said. "Driveshaft. Ever hear of it?"

Jeff shook his head. "Maybe some of my students did. I'm afraid my musical taste runs to classical. You know, the four Bs—Bach, Beethoven, Brahms, and the Beatles."

Charlie said, "Well, we weren't quite in their league. But we didn't do too badly. Not too badly at all."

Michael looked at Jeff carefully and said, "I don't mean to pry, but how is it that you don't know that? I mean, this guy chatters about Driveshaft to anybody who'll listen."

"Am I as bad as all that, then?" Charlie said.

"Yes," said Michael.

Jeff walked for a while without speaking. "I don't know how to explain this properly," he said. "Even to myself. But ever since we've been here I've just felt . . . removed. There's no other way to put it. I haven't wanted to meet anybody or talk to anybody. And when I found my studio, it just seemed like fate had provided a place for me to be alone."

Michael said, "Well, you seem like a friendly enough guy."

"Yeah, except for the whole mysterious loner vibe," Hurley said.

Jeff laughed. "I am friendly," he said. "At least, I always was before this, I think."

To his surprise, Jeff felt comfortable with this little group and eager to get to know them better. When Michael asked him about his art life back in Great Britain, Jeff regaled him with stories and described his various exhibits and adventures. He asked Michael about his work and listened with great interest as Michael told him about the kinds of things he drew and the kinds of things he aspired to draw. As the talk went on, hour after hour, as they hiked across the island, Jeff began to realize how much he had missed having human contact, having friends.

This is fun, he said to himself. *Or, as Mr. Blond would say, Very nice, very nice, very nice.*

The only member of the party who didn't involve himself much in the conversation was Locke. He stayed a distance in front of the others, carefully searching the trail for signs that a boar or some other edible animal might be in the area. Every hour or so, he signaled for them to stop and rest. When he did, they sat on the grass, leaned back under shade trees, and took cautious sips of water.

It was still well before noon, but Hurley declared that it was time for lunch. They each took a piece of fruit from their packs. Michael had brought two leftover fish from the night before, wrapped carefully in a piece of cloth. Charlie was a vegetarian and didn't want any. Hurley scrunched up his nose in disgust at the sight of it.

Michael shrugged, smiling. "Oh well, Jeff. More for us." He handed Jeff one of the fish, then called out, "Locke! We have some fish here! Want some?"

Locke was at least a hundred yards away, standing on a rise and surveying the region before them. He waved his arm "no" and then turned his attention back to the landscape. He was too far away for Jeff to see any expression on his face. *So why,* Jeff wondered, *do I have the feeling that he's worried about something?*

The fish was lukewarm and had not been cooked terribly skillfully, but it seemed like a feast to Jeff. He thought that this was partly simply because he was so very hungry. But there was another reason, too—the fare was made more delicious by the fact that he was having a meal with friends, something that he hadn't done in a very long time. It was a good feeling.

After he ate, Jeff closed his eyes. His lack of sleep the night before was beginning to wear on him and he thought if he could just rest for a few moments, he would be energized enough to continue the journey.

He was jolted awake by Locke's voice. "How long has he been asleep?"

"I'm not asleep," Jeff said defensively. Then he noticed the others were grinning at him.

"If you weren't asleep," Charlie said, "you obviously feel that snoring is a good way of communicating. Because you were singing out!"

"Yeah," Hurley said. "If there's a boar around here, you probably scared him off. He probably thought it was a lion roaring."

Even Locke looked amused. Jeff grinned sheepishly. "I didn't get much sleep last night."

Michael said, "Don't worry about it. You've only been out for forty-five minutes or so. We couldn't go anywhere until Locke got back, anyway."

"Yeah," Hurley said to Locke. "Where ya been?"

Locke pointed ahead, to the place where Jeff had earlier seen him standing. "I saw some boar tracks leading into that little valley just beyond the rise. There might be four or five of them, so we have to stay alert."

Everyone nodded soberly. They all knew how dangerous wild boars could be.

"It's about noon," Locke said. "If we don't bag one in the next two hours or so, we'll probably need to make camp for the night. I think we're past the point of no return. Everybody okay with that?"

Hurley smiled and said, "And if we aren't?"

Locke pointed behind them. "You know the way back to camp."

Hurley, Charlie, and Michael laughed. "Yeah, right," Michael said. "Like we could find the way back without you."

Locke stood up. He had that friendly smile on his face that Jeff found so unsettling. "Then I guess we'd better press on."

The others stood up more reluctantly. "Forward, march," Charlie said.

They did not find a boar in the next two hours, or in the next four. The sun was beginning to sink below the tree-tops, casting the landscape around them into soft shadow. Without flashlights or torches, they wouldn't be able to continue after dark, so the group's hunt shifted from boars to a place to make camp.

"Let's head over to that hill," Locke said. About a mile in the distance stood a rocky hill which looked to be about fifty feet high. There was not much vegetation growing on it, so it stood out in stark relief against the green coun-tryside. Locke continued, "There might be some over-hangs there. That might come in handy if it starts to rain."

In fact, it rained almost every day; it was just an ac-cepted fact of life for the island dwellers. But even though they were used to it, nobody wanted to sleep in the rain if there was any alternative.

The group turned toward the rocky hill, but before they had taken more than a few steps, four deafening cracks sounded in quick succession. The five men were puzzled and began looking for the source of the sounds. To Jeff they sounded like someone had snapped four broomsticks into the microphones of the loudest sound system on earth.

Charlie pointed to the woods just west of them. "Look!"

As they watched in horror, four huge trees crashed to the ground in sequence. The sound was heard again. Then again. And again. Each time, trees fell with a powerful BOOM! It made no sense, but Jeff was filled with the dreadful idea that something was striding through the jungle, knocking trees down with every step.

That's crazy, he said to himself. *It would have to be huge!*

The men were rooted to the spot for a few seconds, frozen in shock and fear. Locke shouted, "Snap out of it! Let's go!"

They began running desperately toward the rocky mount. They had little reason to believe that it was any safer there, but at the moment it was the only place that even offered the promise of hope.

Jeff sprinted like a long-distance runner. Just as during the crash, he felt somewhat apart from his body, as though his physical self were carrying a watchful spiritual self on its shoulder. The calm "other" Jeff noticed with admiration that Hurley, nearly as broad as he was tall, was actually surprisingly agile; he was keeping up with the others with seemingly little effort. *Amazing,* Jeff thought, *what a little terror will do for you.*

Charlie and Michael wore expressions of pure panic.

Locke simply looked determined. He glanced back occasionally, as if making sure that everyone was keeping up. That gesture made Jeff admire him a great deal more than he had previously. It seemed to indicate a level of responsibility and leadership that did Locke well.

But while Jeff's mind occupied itself in musings and observations, his body remained keenly aware of the danger that lay behind them. The crashing of trees was now mixed with another kind of thunderous roar. It sounded like the pounding footsteps of some horrific giant beast. Jeff conjured up nightmare visions of what it might be, helped along with images implanted by countless monster movies. Was it King Kong? Godzilla? Gorgo?

Locke reached the hill first and immediately began clambering up the rock wall. Michael got there next and Jeff followed in a second, slightly beating Charlie to the wall. Once he was a few feet off the ground, Jeff forced himself to look back. He could see no monster in the increasingly dim light, but everywhere he saw the evidence of its presence. Bushes were flattened, trees felled, and a wide swath was cut through the tall grass by what must have been feet the size of Humvees. The ghastly roaring continued through it all. It sounded like the combined cacophony of a hundred zoos, all screeching to the sky in one thunderous chorus.

"Keep climbing!" Locke yelled. Jeff could barely hear him over the roar of the beast. Climbing furiously, trying to beat down the panic threatening to overwhelm him, he glanced around to make sure that everyone had made it this far. The soles of Locke's shoes were just inches from Jeff's face and he blinked as dust peppered his eyes. Just below his own feet, Charlie and Michael were climbing side by side. Farther down the cliff, Hurley struggled to clamber up behind his friends; the strain was showing on his face as he searched frantically for each foothold.

Jeff turned his face forward again, squinting his burning eyes against the cloud of dirt generated by Locke's efforts. And it was at that instant that he heard a shout from below. Whirling around, Jeff saw that Hurley had lost his footing. Clawing desperately at the rock wall, Hurley grimaced in agony as his body scraped down the cliff.

The unseen beast's roaring was louder than ever and Hurley fell directly into its path, screeching like a man who had fallen headfirst into Hell.

9

JEFF AND SAVANNAH WERE alone in the sitting room of Jeff's rustic little cottage. They spent nearly every Saturday and Sunday there, sketching, painting, making love. They sometimes spent hours together without saying a word, he standing at the easel that he had placed just under the large skylight, she curled up on the daybed, working earnestly at her sketch pad.

When they did talk, the subject was often art. Jeff had been both surprised and thrilled to find that Savannah had not only a passion for art history and technique but a broad knowledge of both; she had quite obviously delved far deeper into the subjects than had any of her fellow classmates. She was articulate and thoughtful, too, and if sometimes her arguments seemed designed just to annoy Jeff, they delighted him for that very reason. He had been accustomed, over the course of his growing fame, to a certain amount of deference, even adulation. But from the moment they met, Savannah treated him as an intellectual equal, albeit one who had things to teach her.

They almost never worked in Jeff's studio at the college, although it was far superior in terms of both space and lighting to the low-ceilinged room they were in now. But the college did not afford them the privacy that they required for these sessions; not simply the privacy that allowed them to make love whenever the idea presented itself, but also the sense of aloneness they required. They reveled in being with each other and no one else.

Besides, Jeff preferred home to almost anywhere else he could think of. Back in London's swinging scene, he was out every night, almost always with a different woman. He was a familiar face at the trendiest restaurants, bars, and clubs and was always on the A-list for the best parties.

But now, even when Savannah wasn't with him, Jeff reveled in his cottage. He loved curling up near the fire in his overstuffed chair, enjoying a glass of wine or a cup of tea. His favored reading at times like these were the great ghost stories of Henry James, Sheridan Le Fanu, Edith Wharton. Among the few pleasant memories of his childhood on the island of Arran were the times when his wizened grandmother, who always looked at least two decades older than she actually was, would terrify him with "true" ghost stories that she had been told when she was a child. All of them took place on the stormy coasts of Scotland or in the castle ruins that dotted the landscape. That delightful frisson of fear was something Jeff came to treasure, and he happily recalled alternately screaming with laughter and squealing with terror at the tales the old woman told him.

Savannah loved these stories, too. He knew that he had found the rarest of women when she snapped a book shut late one night and declared that Oliver Onions's "The Beckoning Fair One" was the finest ghost story in the English language, an appraisal with which Jeff could find no fault.

In fact, on just about every level he could think of, Savannah struck Jeff as being pretty nearly perfect.

Looking back on it, Jeff couldn't quite pinpoint the moment when they became a couple. He was smitten with her before she had finished uttering her second sentence to him and it somehow seemed that she had appeared in his classroom that day for no other reason than for him to fall in love with her.

All the familiar warning bells went off in his head that day, and he heard them clanging every day thereafter. Jeff was very much a man who enjoyed playing the field, and the attractive combination of his profession, personality, looks, and success had ensured that the field was virtually inexhaustible. He had a firm rule about permanent relationships—they were to be avoided at all costs. Affection was nice and sex was a necessity, but "true love" only led to trouble. He had watched helplessly as his parents struggled through a bleak and loveless marriage that drained them both of life and hope; he had witnessed countless variations on that theme with other friends and acquaintances. He found that the beginning part of a relationship was always the vital part—electricity, passion, that vibrant curiosity about one another. But once matters settled into the mundane, passion died and animosity began growing. The solution to Jeff seemed simple—always make sure that the romance never got beyond that exciting opening stage. Clip it off in full bloom and then move on to the next blossom before the inevitable wilting began.

Those warning bells urged caution on another front, too—Savannah was his student. At twenty-two she was legally a consenting adult, but Jeff knew that there were conventions and prejudices in colleges that went beyond clear-cut matters of law. A professor who dallied with a student might find his reputation impugned and his ethics called into question. As artist-in-residence, Jeff wasn't a true member of the faculty; that might give him a little leeway when it came to this kind of behavior, but it would also make it easier for the college to simply wash its hands of him if it disapproved of the way he conducted himself.

Jeff paused, his brush lightly touching the canvas, and gazed at Savannah across the room. Her forehead was knitted in concentration. She was dressed in jeans and an oversized sweater. She hated wearing shoes, and her feet were clad only in thick woolen socks dyed a truly objectionable shade of lavender. He thought she was about the most beautiful sight he had ever gazed upon. While the warning bells tolled ceaselessly, Jeff told himself he just didn't care. Whatever happened because of his affair with Savannah would be worth it. And as he ignored the warning bells, he also ignored that tiny voice in the back of his head, the one that insisted repeatedly, *You're getting in too deep. Enjoy her, and then cut her loose. Don't get trapped. You'll live to regret it.*

But even while a part of Jeff wanted to assert that the relationship had no future, and no matter how many times he told himself that this was nothing more than a highly enjoyable fling, Jeff knew better. He had recognized from the beginning, albeit reluctantly, that Savannah meant more to him than any other woman he had ever known. Her sweetness and openness, her directness of manner, her endless curiosity about the world—all of these elements, combined with her ethereal beauty and powerful, earthy passion, caused her to burrow deep inside his heart. When he was with her, he wanted nothing more than to bask in her presence forever.

And when they were apart and he could think more dispassionately, the dissenting voice in his head spoke louder, making Jeff fear for the loss of his freedom. *No, he told himself then, I could never bear the chains of a lifetime commitment.*

Jeff set his brush down, walked across the room, and sat beside her on the couch. He tried to take a look at what she was drawing, but she immediately clasped the pad to her chest.

"No!" she said. "I'm just sketching nonsense. This is not for public consumption."

"Oh, please . . . ," Jeff said in a mock-wheedling voice. "Just one little peek . . ."

Savannah shook her head firmly. "No! Go back to your own hackwork and leave me to mine."

Jeff stretched out on the couch and settled his head in her lap. She put the sketch pad face down beside her and began gently stroking his hair.

"Speaking of your own substandard art," she said, "what are you working on?"

"Oh, you won't show me yours but you want me to show you mine," Jeff said.

Savannah smirked. "Well, as much as that statement reeks of the schoolyard, yes, I do."

Jeff stood up. "Okay," he said. "Just to prove that I'm the open one in this relationship, and not the secretive, mysterious, possibly evil one, I'll show you."

Savannah followed him over to the canvas. When she saw the painting in progress, she smiled. "Why, it's me!" she said, pretending to be surprised.

"Yes, damn you, it's you," Jeff said. He stood behind her and wrapped his arms around her waist. "Ever since you intruded on my peaceful life, I don't seem to be able to paint anybody or anything else."

She nodded. "That's a good thing. I know all about you famous artist types, with the endless succession of naked hussy models."

"You have the wrong idea about me," Jeff said. "I came to this college straight from the abbey where I spent decades in celibacy and prayer."

Savannah nodded. "So you're saying that if I were to

become naked right this minute, you wouldn't have all kinds of dark and sinister designs on me."

Jeff spun her around in his arms until she was facing him. He began kissing her neck. "No, I'm not saying that at all. . . ." He tugged her sweater up over her head. She wore nothing underneath. "In fact, a dark and sinister design just came to me."

They kissed deeply. As Savannah began unbuttoning his shirt, she said, "Oh, professor! I'm beginning to think you don't have art on your mind at all."

Later, they lay on the couch, covered by a scratchy old blanket. Her sketch pad lay on the floor, having been unceremoniously tossed there while its owner had her mind on other things. For a while, neither of them said anything, but only gasped for breath, recovering from what Jeff considered to be the almost superhuman ferocity of their passion. He had never met anyone even remotely like her.

At length, Savannah spoke. "Have you ever read *Wuthering Heights*?" she asked.

"What an odd question," Jeff said, smiling.

"Not so odd," she said. "I've been reading it recently and I was just thinking about it. It's all grand passions and love that extends beyond death—that kind of thing."

"Yes," Jeff said. "I read it a long time ago. I have to admit I know the film much better."

"Ah yes," Savannah said. "Merle Oberon, Laurence Olivier. That glorious, glorious music. I've loved that film ever since I first saw it on the telly when I was a child. I guess that's why I decided to read the book. Actually, turns out the book's better. Even without the music."

"They usually are," Jeff said.

Savannah reached up and gently caressed Jeff's cheek. "It just got me to wondering, that's all," she said.

"Wondering about what?"

"Well, I wonder if when you die your love will prove stronger than death and you'll come back to me, calling my name in a snowstorm," she said.

"I wouldn't dare," Jeff said. "What if I caught you in an intimate moment with your new boyfriend?"

"Which one?" she asked. "The trophy boyfriend that I'll use on the rebound or the incredibly wealthy playboy porn-star boyfriend who will be the father of my children?"

Jeff chuckled. "Now that you mention it, I don't know that I'll feel very comfortable about either one."

Savannah turned to face him, propping her head on her left fist. "I'm serious."

"What?" Jeff said incredulously. "You're serious about whether I'll be a ghost going boo in the dark?"

"No," she said, a grave look on her face. "I'm serious about wanting a love that will exist beyond death, beyond time. Do you think such a thing truly exists?"

No. I emphatically do not, he thought.

"Well, of course I do," Jeff said soothingly. "Of course I do."

Savannah kissed him lightly on the cheek and stared deeply into his eyes. He found it difficult to meet the intensity of her gaze. She said, "I hope so, Jeff."

Jeff sat up, thinking it best to change the subject as quickly as possible. He said, "May I see your sketches now?"

Pretending to be indignant, Savannah said, "Oh, so you think if you favor me with your sexual prowess, I'll then do anything you ask?"

Jeff nodded. "Pretty much," he said.

She reached down and picked up the sketch pad. "Oh well," she sighed, "when you're right, you're right." She handed it to him.

What he saw on the oversized pages surprised him. Savannah had been devoting much of her work to studies of anatomy, feeling that the human figures she drew and painted were insubstantial. It was not realism she was after, but believability, and she had sought Jeff's help conquering the problem.

But the drawings here were not of humans. Indeed, Jeff was not at all sure that they were anything he had ever seen before. The pages were covered with strange designs. Within some were images of snakes and scarabs. No, on second thought, they were not quite images but suggestions of these things. The pictures were intricately detailed and must have taken Savannah hours upon hours to execute. Jeff thought they were exquisitely beautiful but somehow disturbing.

He stared at the pages for so long that Savannah finally asked, a note of worry in her voice, "Do you hate them that much?"

Jeff shook his head, almost as if he were coming out of a trance.

"No, I don't hate them at all," he said. "They're quite wonderful. But what are they?"

Savannah shrugged. "You tell me," she said.

Jeff said, "I've never seen you do anything like this. Where did they come from?"

Savannah took the pad from his hands and peered at it, as if seeing the drawings for the first time. "I have no idea where they came from," she said. "Just one morning I woke up and started sketching and there they were."

"They're quite amazing," Jeff said. "They look like . . ." He paused for a moment, groping for a way to put his thoughts into words. "They look like hieroglyphics from a civilization that never existed."

Savannah smiled and said, "Don't be too sure."

"Well, if you ever learn to read them," Jeff said, "be sure to let me know what they mean."

Savannah chuckled deeply, like a villain in an old mystery. "It may be that you will learn to read them before I do," she said, doing a very bad Bela Lugosi impression. "And what you find will be . . . horrifying!"

"Oh, trust me," Jeff said with a broad smile on his face, "I'm already horrified."

Savannah shrugged off the scratchy old blanket and wrapped one leg around Jeff's waist. "And you have reason to be."

Jeff reacted with exaggerated shock. "Again?" he said. "Don't you know I'm a rapidly aging academic? I don't know if I can manage it again so soon. I'm very fragile."

Savannah began to caress him softly and glanced downward. She said, now doing a terrible Greta Garbo impersonation, "Your voice says no, no, no, but your body says yes, yes, yes!"

Jeff had to agree that there was a great deal of truth to what she said. They kissed passionately.

"Savannah," he said, his voice husky with desire, "you're going to be the death of me."

She laughed again. That tinkling, musical laugh that he loved so well.

"Nonsense, Heathcliff," she said. "I'm going to save your worthless life."

10

HURLEY SEEMED TO BE unconscious at the foot of the cliff. As quickly as he could, Jeff climbed back down. As he passed Michael and Charlie, they looked at him in puzzlement for a brief moment before beginning to backtrack themselves. Locke, nearly at the top of the precipice, noticed their absence right away. In an instant, he started back. To Jeff's astonishment, Locke actually beat the other three to the ground. *Well,* Jeff thought, *in a surreal world, surreal things happen.*

The four men surrounded Hurley's inert body, unsure of what to do next. The cacophony made by the invisible beast was ear-splitting, but it seemed to come from no specific direction. The men knew that they were just seconds away from contact with the thing and now they were all just sitting ducks.

"We've got to get out of here!" Locke shouted.

Jeff thought that was the most stupidly obvious thing he had ever heard. In a different situation he would have made a snide remark in reply, but being moments away from a horrible death had a way of squelching irony.

Jeff knelt beside Hurley. "Hang on!" he shouted over the roar. "Just hang on!"

Hurley may have tried to respond, but all that came out was a strangled gargle. His face was covered in blood. With each breath he took, crimson bubbles flecked his lips.

Jeff's mind was racing: *What do we do?*

To his amazement, there was an even louder, enraged roar and Hurley abruptly stopped and lay still.

Jeff crawled close to him and whispered, "Are you all right?"

Locke grabbed one of Hurley's arms and started tugging. "There's no time for talk. We've got to get out of here."

Instantly, Charlie and Michael were there, helping Hurley and Jeff to their feet. Hurley's face was terribly scratched and his shirtfront was in shreds, but from a quick glance, Jeff determined that most of the injuries were minor, if painful.

In a hoarse, low voice, Hurley said, "I'm okay. Let's go."

Hurley's arms were draped over Locke's and Jeff's shoulders and Charlie and Michael stayed close to offer additional support. In this awkward bunch, they ran as fast as they could back to the rock hill, now about a hundred yards away. Before they had covered half the distance, they heard the frightening roar behind them.

Locke yelled to Michael, "Help Hurley." Michael ran to Hurley's side and helped him to his feet. As they ran toward the rocks, Locke's hand closed around the butt of his pistol, but he couldn't bring himself to pull it out and fire. As the invisible fury approached, he turned and followed the others to what he hoped was safety.

When they reached the rock face Charlie said to Hurley, "Can you climb?"

Hurley smiled weakly. "Try and stop me."

But before they could start, Jeff spotted something. "Look!" he cried. At the base of the mound, nearly covered by a thick bush, there was an opening in the rock, about three feet high.

Immediately, the four men pushed past the bush and crawled in, hoping desperately that the opening was large enough to offer all of them a safe haven. Jeff stood outside until Locke arrived. "Come on!" he shouted, then ducked through the entrance. Seconds later, Locke leapt through after him.

It was pitch-black inside. Carefully, Jeff stood up. He reached his arms high above his head but still didn't touch the ceiling.

"What the bloody hell was that?" Jeff croaked in a hoarse whisper.

No one answered.

"Well?" Jeff said. "Could anybody make out what it was?"

After another long pause, Charlie said, "We've never been able to make out what it is."

"You mean you've seen this thing before?" Jeff said. "All of you?"

Michael said, "Well, not *seen* exactly. But yes."

Locke's voice sounded in the darkness. "Let's move as far inside as we can. Whatever that thing is, I don't think it can fit through that opening."

Jeff felt like he was losing his mind. "You've encountered it before? What is it?"

"Good question," Locke said calmly. "Now, everybody grab onto somebody else's arm. We don't want to leave anybody behind."

Forming a human chain, they advanced cautiously into the darkness. Jeff was surprised to find out how deep the tunnel seemed to be. He also noticed that there was a distinct breeze coming from inside somewhere.

"Feel that?" he said.

"Yeah," Michael said. "There must be another entrance somewhere down here."

"Hold on," Locke said. And then, with a scratch and a whiff of sulfur, the chamber was filled with dim light. Locke carefully held the lighted match in his right hand and a thick, misshapen candle in his left. When the wick was lit, he lifted the candle over his head.

Charlie chuckled. "Leave it to you to come prepared."

Jeff said, "Yes, that's great—but where in the world did you get a candle? There wouldn't have been any on the plane."

Locke smiled. His eyes glinted in the candlelight. "That's another gift the boars give us. I render the fat to make tallow. If I only had some lye, I could make soap, too."

"Lovely," Charlie said. "Bathing in pig fat."

Michael said, "Now that we can see, let's check Hurley out."

Hurley had been leaning against the wall and began to slide downward into a sitting position. Jeff knelt beside him. Locke held the candle close to his face. Michael took the piece of cloth in which he had wrapped the fish and dampened it with water from one of the plastic bottles. Carefully, he wiped the blood from Hurley's face, pausing two or three times to rinse out the cloth.

"Let's get this shirt off," Jeff said.

"Aw man," Hurley said.

"What?" Charlie asked.

"Dude," Hurley said. "I don't like to take off my shirt in public."

Jeff smiled. "This is no time for modesty. We have to see if you're hurt."

"It's not modesty, dude," Hurley said.

But he allowed Jeff to lift his T-shirt over his head. Hurley closed his eyes, his face red with embarrassment. "Hey," he said. "No fat jokes, okay?"

Jeff quickly crossed his heart with his index finger. "You have my solemn promise. What happens in the tunnel stays in the tunnel." Jeff wet the cloth and repeated his ministrations over Hurley's torso.

"Nothing but superficial bruises and scrapes," Jeff said after a few moments. "You're a lucky man."

"Speaking of which . . . ," Locke said. Everybody looked at him. "Haven't you noticed we haven't heard a thing since we got inside?"

The other four listened carefully. A short distance away, a tiny glow of light surrounded the tunnel's opening, but they saw no savage claw pawing through it. Jeff thought, *This must be what the mouse feels like when he knows the cat is lurking about just outside.*

"Maybe it's gone away," Charlie said.

"Maybe," Locke said, without looking convinced. "But since we feel that breeze, I think it would be a better idea to continue in that direction for a while, see where this thing comes out."

Jeff nodded. "I agree. This place is so narrow, it shouldn't be any trouble to find our way back out again." He knelt beside Hurley. "Are you up to doing a little bit of traveling?" he asked.

"Sure," Hurley said.

Locke doused the candle and instructed everyone to keep one hand on the shoulder of the man ahead of him and the other hand on the wall. They wouldn't be able to travel very fast that way, but at least they would stay safely together.

The little human train continued its journey through the darkness for the next hour. Conversation was kept at a minimum, as each man strained his senses to listen, sniff, or even *feel* anything unusual or dangerous. When they did speak, they kept their voices as low as possible, as if afraid of being overheard. Occasionally someone would remark on the breeze, which wafted through the chamber with increasing power.

"I keep hoping we'll see the light from the entrance," Jeff whispered.

Two bodies ahead, Locke answered, "It's night."

Jeff almost laughed. "Oh, right. I forgot." They had been in the dark for so long that he had no clue as to what time it was.

They walked in silence for another half hour until Locke, at the head of the line, stopped abruptly. "Listen!" he hissed. They all stopped and strained to hear whatever had caught Locke's notice. Jeff heard it at once—breeze wafting through trees. And there was another sound, too—rain. The entrance must be just ahead.

Locke lit the candle again. "Stay here," he said. He walked forward into the chamber and disappeared around a curve. The other four stood nervously until he returned a few minutes later.

"There's an entrance just ahead," Locke said. "We should make camp here. It's raining pretty hard and I don't know exactly where we are."

The others murmured their agreement. Each of them was exhausted enough to just drop where they were. Jeff sat down and pulled his water bottle from the pack and took a long sip. His throat was nearly dry from exertion and terror, and he luxuriated in the intoxicatingly refreshing liquid, lukewarm as it was.

Locke kept the candle lit until everyone had chosen a

place to sleep. The golden light flickered and played on the wall behind him. Jeff thought the swirls and designs of the rock patterns were fascinating—they almost looked like deliberate . . .

Oh my God! he thought. *Oh my God!*

On the wall was a design that was not only obviously deliberately placed there, but quite familiar to Jeff. Reaching into his pocket, he pulled out the wooden talisman he had been carving the night before. Almost in a daze, he stood up and walked over to the wall. As the others looked on in puzzlement, Jeff held the talisman by the side of the carving on the wall. They were identical.

Jeff took a step back and thought once again, *Oh . . . my . . . God.*

11

JEFF WAS SEATED AT the desk in his office, grading papers. This was the most depressing part of his job. He had some gifted fledgling artists in his class and it was a pleasure teaching them new techniques and watching them learn them and adapt them to their own burgeoning visions. At the same time, he was continually shocked at how inarticulate many of them were and what distressingly poor writers. For the art history portion of his lectures, he had assigned essays, and it genuinely pained him to read most of them.

For God's sake! he thought. *They can't spell "Impressionism." They don't even seem to know what it means.*

Savannah's paper was, of course, a different story. She

was as witty, concise, and informed on paper as in the spoken word, and she truly loved learning more about the history of art. She had chosen the pre-Raphaelites as her subject. Jeff wondered if her interest in that odd group developed because he had once told her admiringly that she reminded him of the Lady of Shalott as painted by John William Waterhouse. But, he thought, she probably knew all about the pre-Raphaelites long before he ever mentioned that to her.

The obvious quality of Savannah's paper, and its vast superiority over those of her fellow students, once again gave Jeff a twinge. She would receive an A, and the best of the others would receive Cs. Her excellent grade was clearly earned, and Jeff knew that it was given without bias of any kind. But would others look at it that way?

You see? he said to himself. *This is just the sort of thing you need to avoid.*

There was a soft knock on the door, and Mr. Blond walked in.

"Hello, hello, hello," he said, with what seemed to Jeff to be forced heartiness.

"Mr. Blond," Jeff said pleasantly, also forcing his own heartiness a bit. Since his first day at the college, Mr. Blond had struck him as someone to avoid.

"Is this a bad time, Mr. Hadley?" Mr. Blond said. "I have something rather interesting to discuss with you."

Jeff gestured at a chair. "Please," he said.

Mr. Blond sat down and regarded the stack of papers.

"Ah," he said with a smile. "Grading essays. I hope your students have illuminating things to say."

Jeff smiled grimly. "Yes, the papers are illuminating, but not quite in the way the students intended, for the most part."

Mr. Blond nodded sympathetically. "Yes, I fear we are moving toward a postliterate age. The power of the image is overtaking the power of the word, would you agree?"

Jeff nodded. "I fear there is a great deal in what you say." And, fearful that Mr. Blond would say a great deal more, which was his wont, Jeff quickly added, "But what did you need to see me about?"

Mr. Blond looked a little disappointed that his many thoughts on the postliterate age would have to wait for later expression, but quickly rallied. "You will soon be receiving a communication from the Newton Museum of Art in Sydney, Australia. You've heard of it?"

"Of course," Jeff said. "It's one of the leading museums in Australia."

"They contacted us first about your availability and we assured them that we would by no means stand in your way. By no no no means," Mr. Blond said.

"I'm sorry," Jeff said. "You seem to have skipped over the most important point. My availability regarding what?"

"Oh oh oh," Mr. Blond said. "I see what you mean. I have skipped past the main theme into the footnotes, as it were."

Since Mr. Blond obviously considered this a witty and erudite remark, Jeff smiled appreciatively.

"The Newton wishes to mount a major retrospective of your work," he said.

Jeff now smiled with genuine pleasure. "Well, that is good news."

Mr. Blond smiled back and continued. "But the best is yet to come. They would like for you to, um, accompany the exhibit, as it were. They've asked that you give a series of lectures and master classes in conjunction with the museum's program. And they will offer you quite a handsome honorarium."

"How long would they require me to be there?" Jeff asked.

"Six months," Mr. Blond said. "At the very least."

Jeff frowned slightly. "But if I accept, won't I lose my position here?"

"Not at all, not at all, not at all," Mr. Blond said. "We are happy to give you this sabbatical and will be just as happy to invite you to return to your post at its completion."

Jeff pondered the idea. At first blush, the project seemed to be more trouble than it was worth. The invitation was certainly flattering, but money wasn't a concern, and he liked it here at Robert Burns College.

"I don't know . . ." he began.

The vacuous smile left Mr. Blond's face. "We cannot, of course, insist that you accept the Newton's offer," he said, "but we strongly urge you to, um, under the circumstances."

Jeff stared at him. "What do you mean? What circumstances?"

"We are not puritans, Mr. Hadley," Mr. Blond said. "And certainly a robust young man like yourself may be excused for, er, living life with a certain degree of zest."

"What are you getting at?" Jeff said. But he was beginning to understand.

"Your, shall we say, relationship with young Miss McCartney . . ."

"McCulloch," Jeff corrected.

"Indeed, indeed, indeed, McCulloch," Mr. Blond said. "A relationship of this kind between a student and a teacher, um, it can be . . . misconstrued, let us say, by others who are perhaps not men of the world such as you and I."

"Not that this is any of your business, you pompous braying jackass . . . ," Jeff said, standing up suddenly. Mr. Blond flinched and moved as far back in his seat as he could. ". . . but Miss McCulloch and I are adults and may live our lives as we please. As to any kind of scholastic impropriety . . ."

Mr. Blond waved his hand, visibly afraid that he was about to be punched in the nose. "No such impropriety has been alleged or implied," he said. "But people talk. And I believe you know as well as I do that here in academe, general impression is sometimes more compelling than actual fact."

Mr. Blond rose from his chair and backed toward the door. "All I am trying to convey," he said, "is that this might be the perfect time to accept such a flattering offer as the Newton is about to make. When you return, Miss McCart . . . um, McCulloch will have graduated and then your relationship can be a matter of interest only to yourselves."

He opened the door, but before he left he turned and said, "As for your personal remarks, I will ascribe them to the heat of the moment." He walked out, closing the door behind him.

Jeff sat down. A brief wave of rage washed over him, but he recognized it as his natural reaction to being scolded by an annoying pipsqueak like Mr. Blond. As he began to think more rationally, he realized that the offer from the Newton Museum was like a gift from heaven. He was still ecstatically happy with Savannah—so, by his lifelong schedule, it was obviously time to cut things off. Actually going out of the country immediately thereafter could only help matters. She would be hurt at first, he thought, but if he was not around, she would forget about him soon enough.

And besides, he thought, he had never had an affair with an Australian woman. He began mulling over the possibilities, but suddenly stopped. He didn't want to have an affair with an Australian woman. He didn't want to have an affair with anybody except Savannah.

You see? piped up his inner mind. *More proof that now is the time to end this thing. If you don't, you're looking at romantic lockup—a life sentence.*

When Jeff got home that evening, Savannah was in the kitchen cooking. As he opened the door, she ran to him, throwing her arms around his neck and covering his face with kisses. "You're late!" she said. "Another ten minutes and the spaghetti would be ruined."

"Spaghetti?" Jeff said.

"Oh, yes," Savannah said. "All those rumors about me being a horrible cook are just the talk of jealous minds. I make an amazing spaghetti sauce."

Jeff felt a definite twinge of déjà vu.

"Oh, yeah," Savannah said, hurrying back to the kitchen, "a registered letter came for you an hour or so ago."

The eerie feeling intensified. It was just like that evening three years ago with Ivy. He had been confident that she would take his leaving well, and it had turned into a disaster. Now, faced with making a similar speech to Savannah, Jeff was suddenly petrified.

He opened the letter from the Newton Museum and read its contents. It basically stated what Mr. Blond had already told him.

"What is it?" Savannah called from the kitchen.

Jeff walked in. He tore a small piece of French bread off the loaf and dipped it into the bubbling red sauce. Giving it a second to cool, he ate it. "This is absolutely delicious," he said.

"I know it," Savannah said with a wide smile. "My spaghetti sauce is the subject of song and story. There's talk of sainthood."

"Well, if I get a vote," Jeff said, "you're in. Saint Savannah, Our Lady of Pasta."

She pointed a saucy spoon at the letter. "You never told me what's in the important mail."

"Oh," Jeff said. "Ah. It's terrific news, actually. I've been invited to Australia. The Newton Museum."

"Ooh!" Savannah squealed. "I saw a special on that place on The Discovery Channel. That's wonderful! Congratulations! But why do they want you, of all people?"

Jeff sat down on one of the rough kitchen chairs by the table and poured himself a glass of red wine. "There are those who consider me a great and important artist," he said.

"Yeah, and people go to Andrew Lloyd Webber musicals, too," she said with mock scorn. "No accounting for taste. How long will you be there?"

Jeff hesitated. Now was the time. "Six months," he said. "Maybe longer."

Savannah sat down in the chair next to his. "Oh, that's a long time." Then she smiled. As always, her smile made Jeff think he could be happy looking at nothing else for the rest of his life. "But I can always finish my term when we get back. Who cares if I graduate this year or next? Not me!"

Jeff didn't know what to say. "Well, are you sure you'd want to . . ."

"Am I sure?" Savannah said. "Would I pass up a chance like this? Not on your life, bub! When do we leave?"

Jeff took another deep gulp of wine. "I don't know the precise date," he said. "Not for weeks yet."

As Savannah went happily back to her legendary spaghetti sauce, Jeff poured himself another glass of wine. Not for weeks. On the bright side, that would give him weeks to think of what he was going to tell her.

12

"WHAT IS THAT THING?" Hurley said.

Jeff looked back at Hurley, Charlie, Michael, and Locke with a helpless expression on his face.

"I carved this last night," he said, knowing how insane this sounded. "I dreamt about this thing and I woke up and carved it. That's why I didn't get any sleep. I worked on it all night long."

"Dude . . . ," Hurley said. "Weird."

Jeff sat down on the ground. Charlie wordlessly asked to hold the talisman and Jeff handed it to him. After he examined it for a moment, he handed it to Michael. Then Hurley and Locke took a good long look at it. Shrugging, Locke handed it back to Jeff.

"This is kinda like that stuff you showed me yesterday," Hurley said. "But kinda not."

Jeff was silent for a moment. Then he spoke. "All right, I'm only going to say this because there isn't a lunatic asylum on the island for you to throw me into. You can believe me or not. The artwork I showed you, Hurley . . . I dreamed it all."

The others' expressions didn't change much but Jeff figured that every man there thought he was totally bonkers.

"It started soon after we got to the island," Jeff continued. "At first I thought art was behind me, something I could never go back to. Then one day I woke up and started sketching. The next morning I made a sculpture out of mud and rocks. And then I started carving things. Every day, something different. And every day it was something that I couldn't identify. It wasn't until last night that I realized what was happening. I had a terrible dream, and in that dream these awful creatures threatened me."

"What kind of creatures?" Michael asked.

"I can't say for sure," Jeff said, shaking his head. "I'm not sure if I couldn't quite see them in the dream or if I just can't remember now. They weren't like"—he gestured outside the chamber—"like that. They were probably human, kind of." Then he remembered another detail. His face brightened. "Yeah, they were definitely human, because one of them was a woman. And she held this thing over her head and spoke to me in a language I didn't understand. I woke up immediately and started carving."

He looked around at the group. They were all listening intently.

Jeff continued, "The thing is, as soon as I woke up, the

dream started to evaporate, you know, the way dreams do. But the image of this thing was rock-solid in my mind. I knew I had to carve it then and there. And that's when it suddenly came to me that I'd been having dreams like this for weeks."

No one said a word.

Jeff smiled a little. "Okay, who brought the strait-jacket?"

Locke said, "If you need a straitjacket, then we all do." The others nodded.

"All of us have seen things," Locke said, "experienced things that don't seem to make any sense. What about that thing outside? Ask any of us to make sense of that."

Michael said, "There's something about this island. The ordinary rules don't apply here."

Jeff held the talisman up. "So," he said, "do you think it means something?"

No one answered for a moment. Then Hurley said, "Dude!"

Jeff looked at him.

"Remember yesterday," Hurley said, "when I told you I had seen stuff like yours on the island?"

Jeff said, "Yes, of course."

"I just remembered, dude," Hurley said. "Now I remember where it was."

All eyes turned to him.

"The caves, dude," Hurley said. "I saw this stuff at the caves."

Locke extinguished the candle. "We need to get to sleep," he said.

"Wait a minute," Jeff said. "What caves?"

Locke said, "Go to sleep. We'll talk about it tomorrow."

Jeff lay down in the soft dirt. He placed his pack under his head and it made a passable pillow. The rain still pelted the ground outside and its gentle drumming made a soothing white noise. Jeff's mind was racing with so many outlandish ideas that he was sure he would never go to sleep. But soon he heard Hurley snoring loudly. Then Michael joined in. Within a few seconds, Jeff followed.

But although Jeff found sleep, he did not find rest, for as soon as he was soundly unconscious, the things came again. This night, they were more clearly human than ever before. Jeff thought that they might have resembled druids in hooded robes or some ancient death cult in ceremonial garb. But this was more of a feeling than anything else; the figures remained frustratingly shadowy, like objects glimpsed out of the corner of the eye.

But tonight, they weren't threatening Jeff directly, as he had felt in the previous nightmare. This time they bore on their shoulders a woman—the same woman who had held the talisman the night before. She writhed in their grasp, screaming desperate, terrified screams. As Jeff watched helplessly, they placed the shrieking woman on the ground and surrounded her. To his horror, they pulled out long, sharp knives and as her screams intensified, they knelt beside her, raised the knives high, and then brought them down savagely in thrust after thrust. In moments the area was swimming in blood but the woman's screams did not abate.

But now, the sound Jeff heard was no longer the screams of the unfortunate woman, but the cries of someone else. The figures rose again and turned toward Jeff. One of them held something aloft. It was a newborn baby, covered in its mother's blood. As the figure held the infant high over its head, the others dipped their hands in the pools of blood on the ground and began to paint on the walls of the cave.

The blood was such a deep shade of red that it almost looked black, and the dream cave was dark and murky. But Jeff did not need light to see clearly the designs that the things were painting on the walls. He had seen those designs almost every day since he arrived on the island.

He had created them himself.

13

THERE WERE TIMES IN Jeff Hadley's life when he was simply appalled with himself, and this was one of them.

He let himself in to Savannah's flat that evening after work expecting to take her out to dinner. They had exchanged keys weeks earlier. Jeff had been relieved that Savannah had never expressed an interest in moving in with him and that she seemed to find the current arrangement very much to her liking. Each of them kept a toothbrush and a change of clothes at the other's home and they came and went at will. Savannah's need for a certain degree of solitude matched Jeff's, so they seldom ran the risk of getting on each other's nerves. It was, in short, nearly the perfect setup.

The date of Jeff's departure to Australia was fast approaching. When he had first brought up the subject to

Savannah, it seemed distant, giving him plenty of time to have a mature discussion with her, explaining that now would be the perfect time for them to go their separate ways. But the weeks passed and they never had that talk. Jeff determined that tonight was the night.

But when he stepped inside Savannah's flat he could see from the foyer that her bed was covered with open suitcases beside which sat stacks of clothes.

"If you want a greeting kiss, you'll have to come get it," Savannah called brightly from the bedroom. "I'm neck deep in packing."

Jeff walked over and stood at the door. He struggled to keep a light tone in his voice. "Going somewhere?" he asked.

Savannah laughed. "You never realize how much stuff you'll need for six months abroad until you start trying to load it into little boxes. Perhaps we could live in a nudist colony in Australia. It would certainly cut down on the luggage."

Jeff didn't smile or offer a responding joke, and Savannah noticed immediately. Her face grew serious and she said, "Is something wrong?"

Jeff said nothing. He moved a suitcase to one side and sat down on the edge of the bed. At length he summoned up the courage to say, "We need to talk."

No pleasant conversation has ever begun with those words. Slowly, Savannah stood up and sat beside him on the bed. "What is it?" she asked.

Jeff took a deep breath. He realized that he didn't want

to have this talk, that he didn't mean what he was about to say. What he wanted to say was that he had never loved anyone as he loved Savannah, that all he desired of his life was to spend every day of it with her. But he told himself that this was merely weakness. She was so attractive, so vital, that naturally he was reluctant to split things off. That was the downside of his philosophy of leaving while things were going well—that was the time when it was always the most difficult to leave. But even as that thought flitted across his mind, he knew that it wasn't true. He had never regretted cutting off his prior relationships, because none of those women had ever meant anything to him. But Savannah did. She meant everything. Even as he prepared to speak the words that would break her heart, a voice in his head shouted, *What are you doing? You're insane!*

"First off," Jeff said, his voice hoarse and low, "I want to ask your forgiveness for not having had this talk earlier. I am a coward. I admit it."

Savannah just looked at him, her eyes wide with dread.

"You're not going to Australia," Jeff said, staring down at the floor.

Savannah swallowed hard. Her eyes glistened. "What . . . ?"

"You were never invited," Jeff said. "But you seemed so excited at first that I thought I'd break it to you a little later. And then I just never got around to it. I've been so afraid to hurt you, I suppose I've just ended up hurting you more."

Savannah stood up. She uttered a sharp laugh. "Well, on the bright side, that clears up all these packing woes, huh?"

She paced around the room for a moment, looking at her clothes and possessions stacked everywhere.

"I'm so very sorry, Savannah," Jeff said.

She sat down beside him again and kissed him on the cheek, and then forced herself to smile. "I won't say that this isn't a blow," she said. "But I'll survive. And by the time you return, I'll have composed a really elaborate scolding, which will make your life miserable for weeks at a time."

Jeff continued to look at the floor. A shadow of concern darkened Savannah's face and she ducked her head slightly, trying to look him in the eyes. "What is it?" she asked. "You are coming back, aren't you?"

Jeff nodded. "Yes, I think so. But . . ."

"But what?"

Jeff looked up sharply. *The only way to do this,* he thought, *is to do it quickly.*

"Come on, Savannah," he said. "We've never had any illusions about what this is."

"What do you mean?"

"This has been a wonderful experience, and you're a terrific person . . ."

"A terrific person?" she said, a note of outrage in her voice. "A terrific person? So that's what I am, is it? A jolly good bloke?"

"We both knew that this couldn't last forever," Jeff said, and even as he spoke the words, he knew he was lying.

Savannah stood up, furious. "We didn't *both* know anything of the kind! I love you. I thought you loved me."

Jeff looked at her helplessly. *I do love you. More than anything or anyone in the world.* "Of course I care for you," he said, "but after this long separation . . . who knows what we'll want when it's all over. It's best just to call it quits now."

The anger drained out of Savannah's face. She looked as if she had just been slapped. She whispered, "Quits?"

Jeff stood up. "It's the best thing. We both know it," he said.

Tears began rolling down Savannah's cheeks. "Please stop saying what we both know. Obviously you don't understand a thing about what I know."

"My dear . . ." Jeff said. He gently caressed her cheek. She swatted his hand away.

She said, "What I know is that you're the love of my life. And I know that I'm the one woman in the world for you." She began weeping. "And you know it, too."

Jeff walked toward the front door. "Once I'm gone, you'll forget all about me. You'll find someone you like even better."

Savannah covered her face. Her body shook with sobs.

"I'm so sorry," Jeff said.

He opened the door. Before he stepped out, he heard Savannah say in a low, breathless voice, "You will never live a day of your life without thinking of me."

He knew it was true. But at the moment, he seemed

powerless to change the course of events. He had known it would be difficult; he just had to remain brave.

Jeff stepped out into the hallway. As he closed the door behind him, he heard Savannah's wails of grief as she collapsed among her half-packed suitcases. And he knew that every time he thought of her, he would hear that terrible sound.

14

HANDS ROUGHLY SHOOK JEFF awake. Squinting, he was surprised to find the chamber flooded with light.

"Get up, dude," Hurley said, giving Jeff's shoulders another shake. "Locke's found a boar!"

As Jeff sat upright, he looked at Hurley. His face looked terrible. Its numerous bruises had left a painful design of ugly purple and black patches, and the cuts had become a ghastly road map of dark, dried blood. Hurley was wearing his T-shirt backward, so that the shredded part showed only his back, but Jeff assumed that his chest and stomach looked just as bad.

Hurley saw the way that Jeff was staring at him and smiled a little. "Hey, dude," he said. "You shoulda seen the other guy."

Jeff grinned. "I tried to. I really did," he said.

"Come on," Michael shouted from the mouth of the chamber. "We gotta go!"

Charlie added, "Take your packs. We may not come back this way." Then he ran from the place, hot on Michael's heels. Jeff slipped his pack over his shoulder, grabbed both spears, and went running out just behind Hurley.

Not coming back? he thought. *I need to examine the walls. I have to come back.*

"Over here," Locke called. He was standing at the bottom of a shallow slope that led down from the chamber's entrance. He pointed to a thicket about fifty yards to the west.

When the other four reached Locke's side, he said, "Watch." They all stood motionless, staring intently at the dense growth of bushes and vines. After what seemed to Jeff like an hour—actually it was only three or four minutes—the bushes began to rustle, gently but noticeably.

Locke said, "We've got him but we have to move fast."

"What do we do?" Charlie asked.

"We surround him," Locke said. "We pace it off so that we're equal distances from each other and from the thicket. Then we try to get him to run out."

Jeff said, "And the ones of us he doesn't gore will stick him with these excellent weapons."

Locke nodded. "That's about the size of it," he said. "He'll run toward one of us, so the rest will have to get over there as quickly as possible. It may take all ten spears just to bring him down. I only caught a glimpse of him, but he's a monster."

I've had quite enough traffic with monsters after yesterday, Jeff thought. *I don't want any more.*

Nobody seemed to think very much of Locke's plan. But no one could think of a better one.

Michael sighed and then said, "Okay. Where do we go?"

Locke started walking calmly toward the thicket, motioning the others to follow him. Every time the leaves rustled suddenly, every man except Locke nearly jumped out of his skin. Jeff thought back on how adventurous and exciting this had all seemed yesterday. But now, with the imminent prospect of coming face to face with a huge, deadly wild animal, the entire enterprise seemed less thrilling than suicidal.

Once near the bushes there was no more talk. Locke positioned each man by walking him to his spot and pointing to the ground. Then he paced off twenty yards or so and placed the next one there. When every one was in place, Locke walked around the perimeter of the thicket, miming instructions. Throw the first spear, he demonstrated, then throw the other. To Jeff, the directions seemed easy enough. Just about as easy as getting an angry tusk in your gut from a charging hog.

Jeff, Michael, Charlie, and Hurley stood nervously, each with a spear upraised. Jeff felt both ridiculous and terrified and imagined that the rest felt pretty much the same way. When Locke saw that they were all in position, he held both of his spears in his left hand and then he picked up a large rock in his right. Suddenly, so suddenly that he startled the rest of the party, Locke rushed toward the thicket wailing like a banshee. When he was just a few feet away, he threw the rock into the bushes. As soon as he did so, he began running past Hurley to the opposite side of the thicket, to the spot where Jeff was waiting.

Before he could get there, the boar crashed through the branches with a roaring squeal and thundered directly toward Jeff.

"Stick him!" Locke shouted.

Jeff thought that those were the two most insane words he had ever heard. He was an artist, a scholar, and a gentle lover of women; he was certainly *not* the sort of Neanderthal who could kill a monstrous beast with little more than his bare hands.

But even before the split-second thought had flitted across his mind, Jeff had already braced himself and tossed the spear directly at the boar.

And missed.

The boar lowered his head just as he reached Jeff and then raised it with a savage thrust, tossing Jeff into the air. His body hit the backside of the hog before he tumbled onto the ground and rolled through the tall grass. He struggled to his feet and had time to flash upon the welcome idea that he could stand up at all. He had dropped his second spear in the fall and by the time he found it and stood ready to throw it, he saw that two spears had already found their mark, one in the boar's side and one in his flank. The latter one interfered with the motion of his back left leg and the boar stumbled momentarily. He was running again in an instant, but the delay had just been enough for Locke to unleash his second spear, and for Michael to throw his.

Now the boar was beginning to look like a gargantuan, bloody porcupine. He staggered forward a few more feet, then crumpled down on his front knees. Locke saw Jeff's second spear sticking up in the ground and ran for it, yelling to the others, "Finish him!"

As much pain as he was in, and as much as he knew the killing was necessary, Jeff felt a wave of pity for the boar; he truly felt like a savage, and he didn't like the feeling one bit. Nevertheless, he knew what had to be done. Running up to the struggling boar's side, Jeff thrust his spear with all his strength into its right eye. He was astonished that the point actually found its mark and he immediately jammed the shaft as deeply into the skull as he could.

The pig dropped to the ground with a heavy thud. The hooves twitched and spasmed for a few moments, but Jeff knew the beast was dead. Jeff backed up a few paces, staring at this once-living thing that he had killed, and sat down in the grass.

Well, that's something I never saw myself doing. Life is full of surprises.

Hurley and Charlie still held both of their spears. Both of Michael's had found their mark, as had both of Locke's. Locke stood holding Jeff's second spear. All four of them gazed at Jeff in disbelief.

Locke smiled in admiration. "That, my friend," he

said, "was a solid kill. You never told us you were such a hunter."

Jeff continued to stare at the boar, a bemused smile on his face. He looked up at Locke and grinned widely. "I can't even bring myself to bait a mousetrap."

Charlie patted him on the back. "That was the old Jeff," he said. "Now you're Island Jeff, the mighty boar hunter!"

The others laughed in agreement and each one came by to pat Jeff on the back.

Locke unsheathed his Bowie knife and unceremoniously slit the pig's throat. "We have to bleed her out," Locke said. "Otherwise the meat will spoil." He motioned to a large tree with a sturdy limb about seven feet off the ground.

"We need to get her hung up to finish the job. And that's something I can't do by myself."

"Her?" Jeff said, a queasy feeling in his stomach.

Locke nodded. "She's a sow. I couldn't tell until we got this close."

Somewhere there are little piglets, squealing for their mummy, Jeff thought. *He immediately tried to banish the thought from his mind. Mummy or not,* he thought, *she tried to gut you a few minutes ago. And she's going to feed a lot of hungry people.* Jeff didn't know if that was just a convenient rationalization, and he finally decided he didn't much care. It was done and there was no going back. No point in making it worse by trying to stir up some guilt within himself.

Locke took out a length of rope and began looping it around the sow's hind feet and then motioned for the others to lend a hand. It took the full efforts of all five men to drag the boar over to a tree. Once there, Charlie shimmied up the tree and tossed the rope over the limb. Then Charlie, Jeff, and Michael pulled the rope while Locke and Hurley hoisted the pig. As soon as the boar's snout was a few inches off the ground, Locke said, "That'll do." He looped the rope around the base of the tree several times and tied a sturdy knot. Then he took his Bowie knife and made a long, deep slit all the way down her belly. A thick stream of blood rushed out and pooled on the ground.

Locke said, "We should leave it for an hour or so. There's a spring over here so we can fill our bottles and wash up a little. And there's a tree with some kind of fruit on it. It looks a little like mango, but I don't think I've ever encountered it before."

Hurley frowned and said, "If you don't know what it is, how do you know it isn't poisonous?"

Locke smiled and said, "Life is risk, my friend."

Jeff was grateful to be able to wash up and he was grateful that the fruit turned out to be delicious and no one got sick. After they had breakfasted, they set about building a sled to drag the boar back to camp. They hacked down two long bamboo stalks and used another length of rope to connect them to shorter limbs placed horizontally. The job was made more complicated by Locke's unwillingness to cut the rope into shorter pieces. There was only so much rope on the island and conservation efforts were in order. Michael found some sturdy vines, which helped the process along.

When it was ready, they dragged the sled over to the

tree and positioned it under the boar. Then Locke untied the knot in the rope and all five men helped to lower the carcass carefully.

Locke pointed west. "The beach is over there, maybe a mile. I think it would be easier travel to head that way, and then drag the boar along the beach. Fewer obstacles on the ground."

The other four nodded. Jeff said, "Before we go, now that there's light, I want to check the walls of that place one more time."

"What for?" Michael asked.

"I need to see if there are other designs in there like the one we saw last night," Jeff said. "I need to try and understand what's going on."

Locke nodded. "Well, make it fast. We can get back to camp while it's still daylight if we get out of here pretty soon."

Jeff sprinted back up the hill and entered the chamber. He held the talisman in his hand, ready to compare it to anything he might see. But he saw nothing. His disappointment turned to shock when he realized that even the design he had seen the night before—the one they had all seen—was no longer there.

15

IF JEFF HAD BEEN surprised by the pomp and circumstance of his arrival in Lochheath, he was absolutely shocked by the near-adulation that greeted him in Sydney. During his three years at Robert Burns College, although he had sometimes traveled to London or Glasgow, Jeff had felt rather isolated from the art world. His work had been shown regularly in galleries and museums, but he rarely attended the openings after a while. And his income from sales had increased steadily, sometimes markedly, over the years. But he began to look at all that as slightly abstract and instead concentrated on reveling in the slower rhythms of working in his old Scottish house. He had little social contact outside the school, and that was all he required. After all, he had Savannah.

Because he had cut himself off from the social whirl,

he rather assumed that he had vanished from the public's consciousness. But Sydney proved otherwise. A large contingent of museum dignitaries and fans greeted him at the gate at Sydney Airport and his first week in the city was a whirlwind of television, radio, and newspaper interviews. He was feted at gala dinners, given box seats at the theater and the opera, and generally treated like a rock star.

Every bus stop in town was adorned with a large poster advertising Jeff's exhibit at the Newton. The painting reproduced on the poster was Jeff's sly parody of *The Lady of Shalott*. This meant that every time Jeff walked down the street he was confronted with Savannah's smiling face, rendered in the lush and gorgeous tones of the pre-Raphaelite artists from whom Jeff had taken his inspiration for the painting.

And every time he saw the poster he thought, *What have I done?*

Jeff's exhibit broke all museum records for attendance. He had been a denizen of the art world long enough to know that this kind of popularity was always soon followed by critical backlash. There was, he knew, a tendency—a compulsion, actually—among critics to build up an artist only to tear him down. And so as his greatness was acclaimed repeatedly in the media, he braced himself for the inevitable moment when the critics began cutting him off at the knees.

But that moment never came. His time in Australia was nearly magical in that regard. Everything about it was perfect, except for the fact that he had tossed away his only chance at happiness.

Jeff's popularity brought with it the requisite art groupies. They were not as ubiquitous as those enjoyed by rock stars, but they were usually just as enthusiastic when it came to expressing their admiration. Many of them were would-be artists themselves, and after the amenities of the act of love were concluded, they tended to bring the subject around to their burgeoning careers, inquiring discreetly how Jeff might help them along on their own paths to greatness. Jeff was usually gracious and noncommittal and was always careful that, while he had their phone numbers, they did not have his.

Jeff pursued these casual encounters with even greater fervor than in the past, trying everything he could to banish Savannah's face from his mind. But every woman he met made him think of her. Everything they said made him think of how much brighter she was than they. Every idea they uttered made him remember her insight and wit. And even the most beautiful of them paled beside his golden memories of her perfect face.

When numerous and nameless one-night stands did not make Jeff forget Savannah, he turned to a more serious affair. He met an attractive gallery owner named Brenda, who was both intelligent and successful. She had a quick sense of humor and was a passionate and eager lover. And Jeff, believing himself to have learned from his mistakes, made it clear to Brenda that theirs was a temporary relationship, one that would last as long as he was in Sydney but that would end the day he left. He was relieved when she readily agreed. She assured him that the future held other handsome artists she would like to get to know; Brenda was no more eager to settle into a permanent relationship than Jeff was. He was happy to hear her say it, but a little disappointed at the same time. It was the first time that a woman had told him, in essence, that he would be easy to get over. Savannah didn't feel that way. Savannah would love him always.

Jeff's enormous success in Australia quickly led to offers from galleries and museums from several countries around the world. The offers felt like a godsend to Jeff. As his time in Sydney drew to an end, he began to dread returning to Scotland. Even if Savannah were no longer there, the memories would be. Jeff wondered if he would ever be able to sleep in his bed or have tea by his fireside without thinking of her.

He contacted the university to tell them that he would not be returning for at least another semester. He spoke with Mr. Blond, who seemed disappointed—but not too disappointed—and who assured Jeff three times that he was welcome back whenever he chose to return.

After sifting through the offers, Jeff chose what seemed to be the most agreeable one, in Los Angeles, California. He knew not a soul there and knew nothing about the city, save what he had seen in the movies and on television. That very blankness of canvas appealed to him greatly. There was nothing of Savannah in that vast megalopolis. No memories. Nothing to make him regret, day after day, week after week, his epic stupidity in letting her go.

He booked a flight on Oceanic 815 to Los Angeles. In the final days of his stay in Australia, he found himself avoiding Brenda. Even though the thought puzzled and disturbed him, their superficial relationship was not enough for him. Savannah was on his mind nearly all the time, even entering his dreams. On several occasions he almost broke down and called her. He began to fantasize about bringing her to Los Angeles with him. The fact that there were no memories of her in the city made him want to create some. Jeff longed to see her excitement in a new setting, knowing that all the fresh sights and sounds would stimulate and delight her.

Oh God, Jeff thought. *I've made the biggest mistake in my life.*

16

THE JOURNEY BACK TO the camp was far more arduous than the trip out the day before. They were, after all, now dragging what Locke estimated to be about eight hundred pounds of raw pork. Locke had been correct that the sand of the beach made dragging the sled far smoother, but getting to the beach had taken almost three hours of back-breaking labor. Now, three men pulled the sled at a time, while the other two rested by walking alongside. When he was pulling, Jeff felt absurdly like one of Father Christmas's reindeer, bearing the timeless gift of meat.

Jeff, Locke, and Michael were harnessed to the sled in the early afternoon. Jeff said to Locke, "Tell me about the caves."

Locke shrugged. "Nothing to tell," he said.

Jeff scowled.

Seeing his expression, Locke said, "Don't worry; we can fill you in on all this stuff later. Although I must say, you're probably better off *not* knowing."

Jeff said, "Well, wherever it is, I need to go there."

Locke shook his head. "Absolutely not," he said.

Jeff was astonished. "Absolutely not? And why the bloody hell absolutely not?"

Michael said, "I know it sounds weird, but I wouldn't go against Locke in a thing like this. He's been inside. He knows how dangerous it is."

"But my art was in there," Jeff said. "That's what Hurley said. Something incredibly strange is going on and I have to find out what it is."

Locke said, "Believe me, we can talk about strange things from now until doomsday and we won't cover half of the strange things on this island. Those caves are dangerous. Nobody needs to go there."

Jeff glanced over at Locke. They continued to pull the heavy boar carcass across the sandy beach. "I'll go there. I don't need your permission."

Locke stopped walking and put down the rope. He and Jeff stepped out and Locke motioned for Hurley and Charlie to take their place as reindeer. Once the boar was being dragged forward again, Locke said, "You don't need my permission, but I'll stop you if you try to go. And believe me, Jeff. If I don't get you, the caves will."

Jeff moved down closer to the beach. He slipped his shoes off and walked through the shallow surf, enjoying the feel of the refreshing, cool water on his tired feet.

Still pulling at the rope, Michael wondered if Jeff was

going insane. He knew how much damage stress could do. He had seen it in himself and had watched it consume others. Maybe, Michael thought, Jeff already knew where the caves weres. Perhaps Jeff had been going there all along, painting and drawing on the walls of it. He might not be crazy. Maybe Jeff was just suffering through some kind of temporary delusional psychosis.

A dozen yards away, walking thoughtfully through the surf, Jeff wondered precisely the same thing.

The arrival of the boar turned the island's mood into that of a feast day. Sawyer and Jin constructed a spit onto which the boar was mounted to begin its slow roast over a fire. The five explorers were hailed as local heroes. Many were concerned about Hurley's cuts and bruises, and while Jack cleaned the abrasions on his face with some alcohol, Hurley invented a story about tripping and rolling down a hill. He figured he could always tell the true story later. For the moment, why spoil the party?

Fruit was gathered, sweet potatoes were prepared for roasting in the coals, and some of the more industrious began to decorate the dining area with flowers and palm fronds. As the sun began to sink over the ocean, someone handed Charlie his guitar and he began to sing raucous tunes from the Driveshaft repertoire at first, then softer, sweeter tunes appropriate to the idyllic setting.

Jeff bathed and changed clothes, then wandered back

to the group. It looked like any clambake on any beach in the world—except for the charred wreckage of Flight 815's fuselage that loomed in the background. The island, as he had seen for himself, could be the scene of tension, danger, even horror. But at the moment, the scene was soothing and pleasant, filled with happy people.

Jeff was jolted out of his reverie by an unfamiliar voice. "You guys did a great job out there. Thanks."

He looked up to find a beautiful young woman standing over him. He had seen her at a distance often, usually in the company of Dr. Jack. She was petite but gave off an aura of strength. Her face wore a wide, generous smile, but there was something in her eyes—it might be sadness, or it might simply be regret. At first sight, Jeff wished he had the tools with which to paint her portrait. But, as beautiful as she was, he was a little surprised to find that he did not want her.

She's absolutely gorgeous, he thought. *But she's not Savannah.*

"My name's Kate," she said, extending her hand. Jeff started to stand up but she sat down in the sand beside him before he could.

"I'm pleased to meet you," Jeff said. "I'm Jeff Hadley."

"Yes, Hurley told me," she said. Looking out at the sea, she smiled and said, "It's a little weird that we've never really met before. I mean, it isn't like the population here is so huge."

Jeff nodded. It was very nice being in the company of a lovely woman again and he spent a moment simply enjoying his proximity to her. He said, "Perhaps Hurley also told you that I've tended to keep my own counsel."

"I know how that is," Kate said. "I feel that way myself a lot of the time." She looked at him. "What's the accent? Not Australian?"

"No, this thick burr is pure Scots," he said. "Except for the ten years I lived in London, I've been a citizen of Scotland."

Kate said, "This isn't much like Scotland, is it?"

"There are more similarities than you'd think," he said. "I was brought up on an island. Granted, the isle of Arran is a bit bleaker and rockier than this, but still . . ."

"An island. Ironic, huh?" Kate said.

"Ironic indeed. I was born on an island and now it seems I'll die on an island," Jeff said with a rueful smile.

"Don't talk that way," Kate said, frowning.

Jeff nodded thoughtfully. "I've nothing to go back to even if we are rescued," he said. "So I guess I don't much care if I ever get home or not."

Kate gazed at Jeff with sympathetic eyes, almost as if she felt the same way. Then her face brightened a little, as if she were forcing herself to be positive. "I can see that we're going to have to get you cheered up a little."

Jeff smiled at her. "You'll find it hard to believe, but I actually feel better now than I have at any time since we got here. It's nice talking to people again."

A voice called from down the beach, "Kate!"

Kate said, "It sounds like they need my extraordinary organizational skills." She stood up and dusted the sand off her jeans. "It was nice meeting you, Jeff," she said. "I want to hear more about that other island one of these days."

"Any time," Jeff said, rising beside her. They shook hands again and Kate went back to the cooking fire. Jeff watched her walking away, noting every detail of her attractive body.

God, he thought. *I miss Savannah.*

The boar meat wasn't properly cooked until nearly nine o'clock. The islanders used broad, heavy leaves as plates. His fellow survivors seemed so congenial that Jeff was rather puzzled as to why he had spent so long avoiding them all. He stretched out on the beach, enjoying the sights, sounds, and aromas of the evening. He felt himself dozing off when he heard Michael's voice.

"I brought you some pork," he said, handing Jeff a frond laden with steaming meat.

Jeff sat up and took the meal. "Thanks. What, no gravy?"

Michael laughed. "Yeah, and no apple pie for dessert, either." Michael put his hand on the shoulder of the boy standing next to him. "Jeff, I'd like you to meet my son, Walt."

Jeff shook Walt's hand. "I'm pleased to meet you, Walt. I've seen you with your dad."

Walt nodded. "How come I never saw you before?"

Jeff smiled sheepishly and Michael nudged his son and said with a tone of fatherly warning, "Walt . . ."

"It's like this, Walt," Jeff said as Michael and Walt sat down in the sand. "I guess I've just been keeping to myself a bit too much." He nodded toward the party. A man and a woman were dancing to Charlie's music; it was nice to see. "Now I'm wondering why I did. I guess coming to the island was a bit of a shock to me."

Walt rolled his eyes. "Tell me about it."

The three of them laughed and then were silent for a few moments as they enjoyed their meal.

"My dad told me you're an artist, like him," Walt said.

Jeff nodded. "That's right. I'm a painter."

"A famous painter," Michael said. When Jeff looked at him oddly, Michael said sheepishly, "I asked around. Locke knew all about you. Went to your exhibit in Sydney. He says you're real good."

Jeff laughed. "Locke, pig sticker and art critic!" he said. "I'll have to thank him for the kind words."

Walt said, "Have you ever drawn any comic books?"

Jeff shook his head. "Sadly, I have not," he said.

Walt looked a little disappointed. "Well," he said, "I hope you do someday. Comic books are cool."

"I think so, too," Jeff said. "In fact, in my collection back home, I have an original *Prince Valiant* Sunday strip autographed by Hal Foster."

Both Walt and Michael looked at Jeff blankly.

"*Prince Valiant,*" Jeff repeated. "Classic comic strip. One of the great . . ." He gave up and laughed. "Before your time, I suppose."

Michael said, "Before your time, too, I bet. You aren't any older than me."

"Not in years, maybe," Jeff said, "but far older in terms of bad behavior."

Walt said, "My dad said you have some art here. Did you bring it with you on the plane?"

"No," Jeff said. "I've been making things since I got here, but I'm afraid they're not very good. And they're certainly nothing like what I used to do."

"Can I see some?" Walt asked.

Michael nodded. "Yeah, I'd love to see some, too."

Jeff shook his head. "It's too dark in the studio."

Michael reached into his back pocket and pulled out a flashlight. "Ta da!" he sang.

"Where in the world . . . ?" Jeff said.

"We found a bunch of them in various suitcases," Michael said. "We try not to use them much—preserve the batteries as long as possible. But I figure this is a special occasion."

Jeff sighed and stood up. The other two stood up, too. "All right," he said reluctantly, "but I don't think you're going to like it."

They followed him through the narrow opening of the studio and Michael flipped on the flashlight. All the pieces sat on the ground, leaning against the "wall" of the studio, and Michael slowly rotated the beam around the circle of artifacts.

Jeff saw that Walt was frowning. "Sorry, Walt," he said. "I told you that you wouldn't like them."

"No," Walt said. "I do. They're cool." He looked at Jeff. "If you ever start doing comic books, you ought to make them horror comics."

It had been an exhausting day and as soon as Michael

and Walt left the studio, Jeff stretched out on his pallet and went to sleep. Instantly, he was back in the terrifying dreamscape. The creatures still stood with the baby held overhead and the mutilated body of the woman still lay on the ground in a swamp of blood. More than ever, Jeff wanted to turn and run screaming from the vision but, like always, he was rooted to the spot.

As he stared, gaping in horror, the woman stood up. She took the baby from the thing that held it and cradled it in her arms, a *pietà* bathed in gore. Now something that Jeff had felt in the previous dreams became evident in heartbreaking clarity—the woman was indeed Savannah. The baby was no longer wailing; it appeared to be dead. Weeping silently, Savannah lay the child down on the ground and, gazing directly into Jeff's eyes, extended her arms. High on her arm were tattoos of the shapes she used to sketch. In his dream, Jeff could almost read them, as if the language they represented was becoming clear to him.

But he was immediately distracted from the hiero-glyphics. Further down her arm, Savannah's wrists were crisscrossed by jagged gashes.

When the sun arose a few hours later, it found Jeff already awake, sobbing.

17

HURLEY SURVEYED THE GROUND carefully. The tension was overwhelming. It was a life-or-death moment. One miscalculation and all would be lost.

Sawyer growled impatiently, "Will you go ahead and swing, already?"

Hurley gripped the golf club tightly and made a few tentative swipes down toward the ball. "Patience is a virtue, my man," he said. He pulled the club back and then brought it down in a perfect sweeping arc. The golf ball sailed down the long slope toward a tiny flag in the distance. "Genius!" he crowed, a note of triumph in his voice.

"Genius, my ass," Sawyer said. "Watch and learn."

As Sawyer placed his ball on the tee, a voice called out, "Terrific shot!"

Hurley and Sawyer turned to see Jeff approaching.

Hurley said, "Oh, hey, Jeff. Sawyer, this is Jeff. Jeff, Sawyer." Jeff held out his hand, but Sawyer just nodded curtly and turned back to the ball. "Shootin' here," he said.

Sawyer swung at the ball, knocking it far to the left, where it landed in a copse of trees.

"Crap!" Sawyer said, flinging the club to the ground. He glared at Jeff and muttered, "So much for concentration." Then he picked up the club and stalked off toward the rough. He called back, "It's your shot!"

Hurley shrugged apologetically to Jeff. "It's Sawyer, y'know?" he said. "He's not Mr. Personality."

Jeff smiled. "I shouldn't have interrupted," he said. "But I need to ask you something. Something I don't want anybody else to know about."

Hurley looked at Jeff dubiously. "Aw, listen . . . ," he said.

"No, no, no," Jeff said. "This won't involve you at all."

Hurley started walking toward his ball. Jeff followed close behind. Hurley said, "You want to know how to get to the caves we were talking about, right?"

Jeff was surprised. "Right," he said. "How did you know?"

Hurley said, "Hey, I only *look* stupid."

Jeff protested, "You don't look stupid."

Hurley shook his head. "I was kidding. Jeez, dude. Anyway, Locke would slice me up like that boar if I got in on this."

"I'm not asking you to get in on it," Jeff said. "Just give me directions. I know you've been there."

"What, are you planning on going there by yourself?" Hurley said.

"Yes," Jeff answered. "I have to do it."

"Would it make any difference if I told you that you were a fool for doing it?" Hurley said.

"Hey," Jeff said, smiling. "I only *look* like a fool."

Jeff had assumed that the journey would require a map, and he had brought pen and paper along to help Hurley sketch it out. But the directions were so simple that he had had to write nothing down. The caves were only a mile from the beach, so Jeff figured he could make it there in under an hour, even if he had to slash through thick vegetation on the way. With luck, he could get there and back before anybody—meaning Locke—had even noticed that he was gone.

He spent the rest of the afternoon watching Hurley and Sawyer's increasingly contentious golf game. When Hurley won, Jeff thought Sawyer was going to fling his club into the sea, like a character in a cartoon. He didn't know the conditions of their wager, but losing seemed particularly galling to Sawyer.

He stormed off ahead and Jeff and Hurley walked back in a more leisurely manner. "I would've made a good golf hustler," Hurley said. "Everybody takes one look at me and expects me to suck."

Jeff said with a grin, "Well, I'm forewarned. If we ever play a game, I'll only wager what I can afford to lose."

Hurley said, "How about if I win, you don't go to the cave?"

"Good try, Hurley," Jeff said. "But I'm going. Just do me a favor and keep it under your hat."

"I won't tell anybody," Hurley said. "But I sure wish you'd think this over, dude."

Jeff got little sleep that night. When he awoke before dawn, his first thought was one of surprise that he hadn't experienced one of his nightmares. They had been occurring every night, so why not this night?

Together with Hurley, Jeff had figured out an alternate way to get to the caves by looping around the camp. It would make the trip a little longer but it would lessen the chance that someone would see him walking into the jungle alone. But even adding this detour, the trip promised to be straightforward.

It was still dark when he slipped out of the studio and padded quietly down to the beach. As far as he could tell, no one else was stirring yet, but he frequently looked back, just to make sure that he was leaving camp unnoticed.

When he had gone about a mile down the beach, he reached a small inlet fed by a waterfall about eight feet high. This was the first signpost that Hurley had alerted him to. Jeff turned right and headed into the jungle. By now the sunrise was sending golden rays through the trees and Jeff had no problem seeing where he was going.

He wanted to get back before anyone noticed his absence and frequently edged into a quick trot through the trees. But even as he did so, he chuckled at the irony.

Practically nobody even noticed I was on the island up until now, he thought. *And now I'm worried that they're all running around shouting, "Where's Jeff?" I could be gone for a week and no one would miss me.*

But even though he suspected this was really true, he continued to jog along, eager to get to the place where his mystery would be solved.

I hope . . .

The sun was high on the horizon when he spotted it. From this distance, a few hundred yards away, it looked like a giant rock jutting out of the lush greenery that surrounded it. It reminded him uncomfortably of the rocky mount they had fled to two days earlier, and Jeff began listening closely for any signs that the invisible beast was on his trail again.

But he heard nothing. Then it struck him—he *really* heard nothing. He stood stock still and strained to hear any sound, but he didn't hear even the screeching and squawking of the jungle birds that normally gave the island its 'round-the-clock soundtrack. The eerie silence seemed to deepen the closer Jeff came.

And with the silence came an irrational fear. When Locke warned him against coming here, he had assumed the danger was physical. Now, Jeff wasn't so sure. He was no believer in the supernatural, but this felt like a haunted place to him. It seemed to him that the temperature dropped markedly when he stepped into the clearing.

As unnerved as he was, Jeff was totally fascinated by the sight before him. It was a cluster of caves, nestled by the waterfall. Most of them had small entrances, only a couple of feet high in some cases. But the opening of the cave directly beside the falling water was tall enough for an upright man to enter. It looked so dark and foreboding to Jeff that he could barely summon the courage to go in. But after a faltering moment, he took a deep breath and stepped forward. He had to go in. He had no choice.

Jeff took out the flashlight, turned it on, and aimed it at

the dark interior. Later, he'd have to thank Michael for telling him about the cache of flashlights—this task would have been a lot more difficult without one.

Stepping cautiously, he walked through the cave's entrance. Once inside, he gasped with awe.

The interior was dark, of course. There was also a thick wall of vegetation that had snaked its way through openings or cracks in the cave's walls.

But he didn't see any designs such as the ones Hurley claimed to have seen.

It was then that a sound came from beyond the wall of the cave. It sounded to Jeff like a gust of wind mixed with a groan of agony. It was, he realized with a chill of horror, a sound he had heard in his dreams.

Quaking with fear, he walked toward the wall. Thick vines and leaves obscured it. When Jeff heard the sound a second time, he began ripping away at the vegetation. And carved on the wall was the talisman.

The groan sounded again, louder. It was a gruesome sound and every fiber of Jeff's being urged him to turn and run. But he knew there was an answer here. He knew he had to find out what was happening to him.

Ripping away more of the plants, Jeff noticed another opening. He cleared more vines away, revealing another cave. With each second, the groan sounded again, louder and louder, as if whatever was in there was coming closer.

Jeff wondered if he was dreaming again. Maybe this was why he hadn't had a nightmare last night—because the nightmare was still in progress. In some strange way, the possibility gave him additional courage. He had never been hurt in one of his nightmares. He always woke up. So, obviously, he was safe now.

Unless this wasn't a dream.

Giving one last desperate pull, Jeff cleared away enough vegetation for him to pass through. Jeff had expected the place to be dark and so was shocked to find that it was lit even better than the cave he had just left. Light filtered in through cracks in the south wall of the cave. The size of the chamber seemed completely out of scale with the other cave, almost as if it were of entirely different dimensions on the inside as on the exterior.

With creeping dread, Jeff confirmed what he had feared for so long—the eerie chamber was precisely the same place as the one he had visited in his terrible dreams. Only it was real. He knew for certain now that he was not dreaming—but he was enmeshed in a nightmare.

On the wall just ahead was a mural of elaborate and disturbing imagery. Jeff recognized many of the designs from his own island work, and many more that he had first seen in Savannah's sketchbook. But there was one difference—this horrible artwork was painted in what appeared to be blood.

As he stared at the art, transfixed in fear, he heard a low whispering from deeper in the chamber. Once again the groan sounded. But this time there was something else. With horrifying clarity he heard a woman's plaintive voice. The voice murmured:

"Jeff . . ."

18

JEFF TOOK A CAB to the Sydney Airport and wheeled his single large suitcase into the terminal. He had always tended to be a little anxious about arriving late and missing flights, so he checked the departures monitor in the Oceanic terminal just to make sure that everything was on schedule. He realized with a groan that he had been a bit too efficient in getting ready for this trip and had over two hours to kill before boarding time.

He checked his bag, endured the long security line, which snaked around like a compressed S, and then located his gate in the International Terminal. He stepped over to a book and magazine stand, selected a paperback mystery novel, and bought it, along with a pack of chewing gum. Gum annoyed him under any other circumstances, but during takeoff and landing he had made himself believe that chewing the foul stuff helped to relieve the pressure in his ears. He had also been told that yawning widely would accomplish the same thing, but he always felt a little foolish trying to induce a yawn.

Jeff settled into a chair near the gate, crossed his legs, and opened the paperback mystery. The author was one he always enjoyed and it seemed to Jeff that the better mystery novels were perfect for travel—well written enough to satisfy his urge for good literature, fast-paced and enthralling enough to keep his mind occupied for the course of a flight.

But even though the book promised to be a real page-turner, Jeff remained mired at the opening paragraph. It wasn't that the normally gifted author was off his game, but that Savannah's face intruded over every sentence.

He had replayed their last disastrous meeting over in his mind repeatedly, always trying to convince himself that he had done the right thing. But as each day passed, he became more and more convinced that he was an idiot. He had lost the first true love of his life. *Lost?* he thought angrily. *I didn't lose her—I threw her away!* And all because of some ridiculous rule he imposed upon himself out of nothing more than fear. Now he couldn't bring himself to go back and try to make things right. But he also couldn't bring himself to face the possibility of a life without her. All Jeff knew for sure was that he missed Savannah desperately and that he was likely to be perfectly miserable until the issue had been resolved.

But each time he drew his cell phone from his pocket, he couldn't bring himself to dial. *What is it?* he wondered. *Is it just my stupid pride that keeps me from going to her and admitting I was wrong?*

He paced up and down the terminal, browsing listlessly in the many bland shops and boutiques. He wasn't hungry, but he bought a cranberry muffin and coffee at a kiosk, just to have something to occupy him for a few moments. Several times he opened the book again and began to read but even the few times that he reached page two, he had to stop and realize that he hadn't retained a single word.

Finally, with great relief, Jeff heard the announcement that Flight 815 was ready to board. He took his place near the front of the queue, boarding pass in hand. The gate attendant passed it through the scanner and gave the stub to Jeff. Later, once he was stranded on the island, he sometimes tried to remember noticing any of his fellow survivors when they were boarding and getting into their seats. But he couldn't. That day, Jeff was too wrapped up in his own drama to pay attention to anyone else.

His seat was on the left side of the aircraft beside the window. There were three seats in each row and with a silent groan of disappointment Jeff saw that he was to be seated in the middle. He was not feeling very social at the moment and sitting in the middle, he felt, just doubled his chances that someone was going to try to engage him in conversation for the duration of the long, long flight.

On the aisle sat a very large man, probably about forty

years old, dressed like a stereotypical tourist and sweating profusely. At the window was a short-statured woman who looked to be in her late twenties. She had a round face that could better be described as pleasant than attractive; she had a rather vacant stare. Her head was topped by a riot of brown curls and she wore a sundress with thin straps.

When Jeff sat down the large man grinned and said, "Squeeze on in, pardner. We're gonna be mighty close for the next few hours." Jeff smiled politely at him and then at the woman on his left. She looked surprised that he had noticed her at all, smiled shyly, and turned to look intently out the window.

Jeff was leafing through the complimentary *Oceanic* magazine, wondering if the crossword puzzle would occupy his mind better than the mystery, when his cell phone rang.

Surprised, Jeff took it out and checked the caller ID. He didn't recognize the number. With a surge of optimism, he thought it might be Savannah, calling from some phone other than her own.

Of course it's Savannah, Jeff thought. *At last. Now I have the opportunity to say everything I've been too cowardly to say before. I can beg her to forgive me, promise her a new start. I can tell her exactly how much I miss her and have been longing for her.*

"Savannah?" he said, a little breathlessly.

There was a long pause. "Mr. Hadley," a male voice said, "Jeffrey Hadley?"

Jeff's hope, however illogical, faded immediately. It was probably just a telemarketer. *Damn them all!* Jeff thought bitterly.

"Yes, this is Jeffrey Hadley," he said with a disappointed sigh.

"Mr. Hadley, I'm Dr. Karlin," the voice said. "I'm calling from Wallace Medical Center in Lochheath, Scotland."

Jeff felt a chill of dread creep up his spine. He said nothing.

"Mr. Hadley?" Dr. Karlin said. "Are you there?"

Jeff closed his eyes and said quietly, "Yes, I'm here."

"Mr. Hadley, do you know a young lady by the name of Savannah McCulloch?"

Jeff began to shake. "What?" he asked, more to buy a few more precious moments of time than for clarification.

"Savannah McCulloch," the doctor repeated. "Your name and phone number were in her purse. There was no other contact information. Are you related to Ms. McCulloch?"

Jeff's head began to pound with terror. "Related?" he said. "Yes. I'm her . . ." *Her what?* "No, no relation. Just a friend. Is she all right? Was she badly injured?"

Now it was the doctor's turn to pause. "I am very sorry to have to tell you, but Ms. McCulloch has passed away."

No! An anguished scream coursed through Jeff's head. *No!*

Or perhaps he actually screamed it aloud. He wasn't sure, but his reaction was strong enough so that the passengers on either side of him jumped in alarm; they both turned to stare at him. Before he could say anything else, the phone went dead. He held the phone in his hand for a moment, staring at it as if it were haunted. Then he quickly dialed the number on the phone's display panel. The call did not connect.

Panicking, he began to get up. He had to get off the plane immediately. But just as he unbuckled his seat belt, a flight attendant leaned in close to him.

"Sir," she said, a blandly pleasant smile on her face, "we're already taxiing down the runway. You must remain in your seat. And please turn off your cell phone."

"But this is an emergency . . ." Jeff said. "I have to get off this plane!"

The flight attendant smiled the patient smile of someone who faces a hundred "emergencies" every flight. "I'm afraid that's not possible, sir. I'm so terribly sorry. But you really do have to turn off your phone."

"But . . ."

"There now, sir," the flight attendant said, her smile growing wider but less friendly, "rules are rules, aren't they? Let's be a good little passenger, all righty?"

For a brief moment, Jeff considered ramping up the incident into a full-fledged argument. That way, he might get kicked off the plane and he could somehow get a flight back to Lochheath. And once he was there, he would find that the so-called doctor was wrong. He had to be wrong. Savannah was just fine. Not dead. Fine.

But he knew that the trip would be useless. Once he arrived in Los Angeles, he could call the hospital to get more details. But why should he? No details would change the cold, horrible truth. She was gone. Gone forever. And he knew that even though he was half a world away, it was entirely his fault.

Jeff sighed again, turned off his cell phone, and slipped it into his shirt pocket. The flight attendant patted him on the shoulder. "Thank you so much," she said. "Oh, and don't forget to refasten that safety belt." Then she moved on to deal with other potential troublemakers.

Jeff clicked the metal buckle of his seat belt and pulled it taut across his lower belly. He leaned back in his seat and closed his eyes. And, to the great concern of the passengers on either side of him, he began to weep.

19

HE COULDN'T HAVE HEARD correctly.

Within the sinister groans emanating from some point just beyond the wall of the chamber, Jeff had clearly heard a voice speak his name. What had previously seemed merely eerie now seemed downright insane. Quickly, he tried to catalog every possible rational explanation—someone was playing a joke on him; someone who knew him by name really *was* in trouble; he was hallucinating; or, that old favorite that he had clung to so often recently, it was only a dream.

But as easily as the explanations came to mind, Jeff dismissed them. This was no dream. It was truly happening. As horrifying, as paralyzing as the thought was, this was truly happening.

Jeff wanted to turn tail and run but some inner

feeling—something between curiosity and madness—
kept drawing him deeper into the cave. Although it was
not too dark, nor was the light fading, something was af-
fecting Jeff's eyesight. Everything seemed to be growing
less clear, as if it were a film gradually slipping out of focus. In some bizarre way, this heartened Jeff a little. He
thought it might be an indication that he was indeed hallucinating and not about to face the flock of otherworldly
demons from his dreams. He had heard of jungle plants
that gave off a deadly perfume with which to trap their
prey. Perhaps some of those plants had grown into the
walls of the cave. Perhaps he was breathing in one fatal
breath after another.

It might kill me, Jeff thought, *but at least it's something I can understand.*

"*Jeff . . .*"

There it was again. Closer now. So close that he began
to tense up, expecting at any second that some gothic creature would burst from the shadows and drink his blood.

But that made no sense, either. Why all these elaborate
clues? Just to lure him, specifically Jeff Hadley, to some
remote place and kill him? No; whatever this was, it was
personal.

Almost as if without a will of his own, Jeff followed
the voices deeper into the darkness.

My God, he thought. *How deep is this place? When I
walked in it looked to be about ten feet wide but I've
been walking for ten minutes and I'm still no closer to
the far wall.*

He squinted at the wall. The ghastly mural was still in

sharp focus, but everything around it was swirling like the oil in a lava lamp. Gradually, with rapidly accelerating horror, he saw that the swirls were alive—those horribly sinister shadow creatures that appeared nightly in his dreams. Their murmuring and groaning were the only sounds in the chamber; Jeff could hear them far better than he could see them. He could sense rather than watch their movements; he knew they were closing in on him. And when he heard the voice again . . .

"Jeff . . ."

. . . he knew, against all logic, that Savannah was among them.

He looked around wildly, belatedly trying to think of some way of protecting or defending himself. They were everywhere, never seeming to move but constantly coming closer. Even this close, he still could not tell if they were human. Jeff figured, since these were the last moments of his life, that he would never know for sure.

Suddenly Jeff felt himself being grabbed from behind. Jeff screamed, a primal scream of pure animal terror, and tried desperately to break away.

"It's me! It's me!" a familiar voice said. His heart still thumping like a jackhammer, Jeff craned his head around and saw that Michael had his arms wrapped around Jeff's chest and was pulling, trying to get him to move back across the chamber to the exit.

Jeff couldn't speak. Michael looked at him with a mixture of concern and fear in his eyes; he clearly thought that Jeff had gone insane.

"We've gotta get out of here, man," Michael urged. "Come on, let's go!"

Jeff stood firmly in place and shook his head. "I need to find out . . ."

Michael pulled again. "You need to leave this place!"

Jeff saw that the creatures were now surrounding him and Michael. He wanted desperately for Michael to let him go. Maybe the two of them could fight together and get out of this alive. But Michael held on tightly, urging, pleading with Jeff to come with him.

Suddenly, with a guttural snarl, one of the things leapt forward and grabbed Michael. Then another and another. Jeff was thrown roughly to the ground and Michael was dragged directly over his prone body, the heels of his shoes kicking Jeff in the nose and mouth.

Jeff struggled to his feet. Within the hazy mob of demons, Michael was crying out with a terror for which there were no words. Just beyond them, Jeff could see that the floor was bloodstained and that there were seven long, sharp blades stuck in the floor, waiting.

Jeff dashed forward but could make no progress through the indistinct mob. It was like wading through thick liquid swirling with savage undercurrents.

The things lay Michael on the bloody spot and surrounded him, picking up the blades and brandishing them over their heads. The groans and murmurs grew louder. Jeff thought it must be some obscene prayer to their devil god. As they chanted, the chamber began to quiver and shake. It felt like an earthquake, but Jeff knew that it was just the upheaval from their unspeakable ritual.

Michael struggled furiously against the creatures, but it was no use. He looked at Jeff with wild eyes, but now when he tried to scream his voice came out only in a hoarse croak. At that instant, Jeff remembered the dream in which the creatures savaged the woman. He knew that Michael was about to be sacrificed, and there was nothing he could do about it.

It was then that he remembered the talisman. *Of course! That was part of the dream, too! It must mean something.*

He drew the object from his pocket and held it at arm's length in front of him. Desperately willing the talisman to exhibit some sort of magical power, he nevertheless felt rather ludicrous, like a character in a Dracula movie.

He half expected the creatures to hiss and retreat from the symbol. But, to his dismay, they paid no attention to it at all. The talisman meant nothing.

He flung the worthless wooden disc to the floor and rushed forward to grab Michael's arm. Pulling desperately to free Michael from the malevolent creatures, Jeff was suddenly aware of another presence.

Savannah stood before him, holding a baby in her arms.

Even in his terrified desperation as he was fighting for his and Michael's lives, Jeff was frozen to the spot.

"Savannah! Oh God . . ."

Her eyes were sad. If Jeff ever could have imagined such a remarkable meeting, he would have expected her to be angry with him, but she looked as if her heart were breaking.

"We could have been everything to you," she said quietly. "We could have saved your life." She spoke in a language that Jeff had never heard. He knew instinctively that it was a language spoken nowhere on earth. Nevertheless, he could understand her perfectly.

The tumult around him seemed to slow. Jeff had the unexplainable feeling that the creatures were curious about this emotional moment, and were watching closely to see how it was going turn out. Somehow, with his mind filled with multiple bewildering ideas, Jeff became aware that the strange earthquake had stopped.

Then all he could focus on was Savannah.

Jeff said, "I'm so sorry . . ."

Savannah pointed to the door. "Protect your friend."

The things had backed away from Michael, who seemed to be unconscious. Jeff stepped toward him and the crowd parted, allowing him to move through them. Jeff knelt to help Michael up but first looked back to Savannah.

"I love you," he said. "I always loved you."

Savannah whispered in the strange tongue, "You have no time."

As Savannah, holding the child, backed away, Jeff began dragging Michael toward the cave's mouth. The other shadow creatures watched him malevolently, their eyes glowing red with rage. Jeff was relieved that Savannah possessed some kind of magic that was too powerful for them.

But he instantly recognized that he was wrong.

Jeff had dragged Michael just beyond the perimeter of the deadly circle when the groaning murmur roared to a feverish volume. As one, the creatures lurched forward as the cave's walls began to shake violently. Jeff could see Savannah beyond the fray, a look of deep sadness on her face. Somehow he knew that she had used all the strength she had, but that it wasn't enough.

Jeff saw Savannah bend forward and pick up the talisman. She placed it in her baby's hands; the infant seemed transfixed by it.

Jeff wrapped an arm around Michael's neck and pulled with all his strength. The cave's entrance seemed to be a universe away, but within seconds, Jeff and Michael reached it and fell through into the outdoors, as something sharp like claws or talons ripped at their backs.

As they collapsed in front of the cave where the adventure began, Jeff turned to see those piercing, glowing eyes glaring through the dark. The things seemed unable or unwilling to cross the border out of the cave. He could hear beyond the entrance that the cave was shaking more violently. Then there was a long, thunderous, rolling crash. Within the roar of the disaster, Jeff could hear unearthly shrieks—hissing, whispered shrieks that were somehow both barely audible and ear-piercing. Jeff pictured the ghastly cave's chamber collapsing in on itself, burying the evil that he had left behind in there.

And Savannah.

A flurry of thoughts rushed through Jeff's mind in the next few seconds, all of them thoughts he would have considered psychotic only an hour earlier. In some part of his brain that remained rational and somewhat detached, Jeff registered the odd fact that the terrible earthquake that had just destroyed the chamber beyond had caused not a quiver in the place where he was now sitting. The low rumbling beyond the wall gradually died away. To Jeff, it sounded less like the quake was stopping than that it was receding.

Jeff undoubtedly would have puzzled over this extremely odd phenomenon for a while longer, except that unconsciousness overtook him just then, and he collapsed beside Michael's unmoving body.

20

JEFF DIDN'T KNOW HOW long he and Michael had lain there on the ground outside the cave. He was the first to come to and sat up unsteadily. His back stung with pain. Awkwardly reaching behind him, Jeff felt his shirt, which hung on his back in shreds. He drew back his hand to find it dusted with dried blood. He looked down at Michael; his arms had several superficial cuts, as if made by long thin fingernails. Michael's chest rose and fell gently and Jeff realized with intense relief that he was alive.

It wasn't a dream, he said to himself in amazement. *It wasn't a dream.*

And that thought led him to another one, both disturbing and wonderful.

Savannah was really here! She spoke to me!

With some effort, Jeff stood up and walked over to the

cave where the entrance had been. It was gone. He felt all around the area, looking for even an outline of the opening, something to indicate that he wasn't losing his senses. But not only was the entrance no longer there—there were only rocks, covered in vines, with nothing else beyond them—he could find no sign that there ever had been a cave.

He walked slowly and painfully and paced. Wherever they had been, Jeff realized, did not exist in the material world.

Of course not, Jeff thought. *How could it be? Savannah was there. She spoke to me.*

Jeff heard a groan from behind him. *Oh God! They're back!* He whirled around, panicked. Then he heard Michael call softly, "Hey, you there?" and immediately relaxed. Jeff walked back over and said, "Yeah, I'm here." Michael had brought himself up on one elbow and was looking around groggily.

Jeff walked over to Michael and knelt beside him. "How do you feel?"

Michael rubbed the back of his head, then stared at the cuts on his arms with some surprise. "That depends," he said. "What the hell has been going on?"

"Don't you remember any of it?" Jeff said.

Michael grimaced. "I remember coming out here to bring you back," he said, struggling to sit up. Jeff helped him to an upright position.

"Nothing else?" Jeff asked.

Michael shook his head. "Nothing," he said. "What happened?"

Jeff said, "I'm still trying to sort that out myself." He put an arm around Michael's waist. "Can you stand up?"

Michael said, "I think so. I'd like to get out of here."

"I know exactly how you feel," Jeff said.

The two men staggered out, using each other for support. Jeff led Michael to a thick patch of grass and gently lowered him there.

"There's a spring right over there. I'll get you some water."

Michael nodded and grimaced. It seemed to him that every single part of his body was hurting. "I just wish you could get me something stronger than water."

"I told you to stay away from this place!"

Jeff and Michael, shocked, snapped immediately toward the sound of the voice. Locke stalked toward them, his face grim.

"What the hell were you thinking?" he demanded angrily.

Jeff stood up to face him. After what he had been through, Locke didn't seem nearly as intimidating anymore.

"I had to come," Jeff said. "I had to find out."

Locke glowered at Michael. "What happened?" he said.

Michael cocked his head toward Jeff and said, "You're asking the wrong guy. Jeff can tell you more than I can."

"I wish that were true," Jeff said. "I can't tell you much. At least, I can't tell you much that would make any sense to you."

Locke continued to glare at him. Then his expression

softened. "We need to get back to camp." Addressing Michael he said, "Can you walk?"

Michael nodded, but didn't look too sure. Locke and Jeff each grabbed one of Michael's arms and pulled him to his feet.

Locke said, "It isn't that far back to camp." He looked significantly at Jeff. "At least it isn't if you don't go the long way around."

Jeff and Michael were not hurt badly, but each felt exhausted. They walked slowly, torturously, back to the beach. Neither they nor Locke said a word throughout their brief journey.

Word had already spread—thanks, no doubt, to Hurley—by the time they got back, and Jack was waiting, wearing a concerned expression, to examine their wounds. And although everyone demanded to know what had happened back at the cave, Locke and Michael could not give any details, and Jeff wouldn't.

What could I tell them? Jeff thought. *That I saw the ghost of the love of my life? I don't believe it myself. How could I expect them to?*

Jack cleaned their wounds and Kate brought some strips of cloth and helped bind a few of the deeper cuts. To Jeff, Kate's presence brought with it more healing power than the bandages; she had the touch of a ministering angel.

"Thank you, Kate," he said when she had finished her work.

Kate smiled. "You owe me," she said.

"What do I owe you?"

"You owe me the full story of what went on out there," Kate said.

Jeff shrugged and said, "When I understand it myself, you'll be the first person I'll tell."

"It's a deal," she said, and moved on to start helping to bandage Michael.

Michael was seated beside Jeff, sipping a broth that Sun had made of seawater, fish, and wild scallions. He leaned over and said, "Thanks, man."

Jeff said, "You don't owe me any thanks, Michael."

"You saved my life," Michael said.

Not me, Jeff thought.

Jeff patted Michael gently on the back, being careful to avoid touching any of the mysterious cuts. He said nothing.

The next morning, Jeff awoke to find bright sunlight streaming through the entrance of the studio. He stretched gratefully; it was difficult to remember the last time he had enjoyed such a long, dream-free slumber.

When he emerged, Jeff saw Walt sitting cross-legged nearby, drawing on a piece of paper in great concentration. Jeff called out, "Good morning, Walt."

Walt waved, and then spent a few more seconds on his drawing before getting up and walking over to Jeff. He held the paper out and Jeff took it. It was a comic-book-style portrait of Jeff as a superhero, holding Michael in his arms as he flew over the island.

Jeff smiled. "What's this?" he said.

Walt replied, "My dad told me you saved his life. He's not sure from what."

"Frankly, I'm not too sure from what myself," Jeff said. He patted Walt gently on the shoulder. "And believe me, your dad is the real hero. He came out there to save me. He would have been in no danger if it weren't for his own bravery."

And besides, Jeff said to himself, *I didn't save Michael. Savannah did. And she saved me, too. Just like she always said she would.*

Walt smiled. "I know my dad's brave," he said. "I made a drawing for him where he's carrying you."

Jeff laughed. "That's very diplomatic of you, Walt!" he said.

Walt cast his eyes downward, hesitated for a moment, and then said, "Will you tell me what happened at the cave?"

Get in line, kid, Jeff thought.

Jeff leaned over a little, so that the two were nearly eye to eye. "I surely will," he said. "As soon as I've figured it out for myself. I promise you that I'll tell you the whole story someday. Okay?"

"Okay," Walt said. He started to walk away, then turned back to Jeff. "Jeff, if it wouldn't be too much trouble, would you give me some drawing lessons?"

"Drawing lessons?" Jeff said, a little surprised.

"I'd like to surprise my dad."

Jeff nodded, smiling. "It would be my honor," he said. "I used to be a pretty good teacher."

Walt smiled back. "Thanks," he said.

Jeff looked fondly at the picture. He considered taking it inside the studio and placing it among his own works. But that didn't seem right. Walt's picture was redolent of optimism, humor, and charm. The works inside the studio spoke to the darkest places in the spirit. He folded the paper carefully and slipped it into his shirt pocket. He would find the perfect place for it later.

21

JEFF STOOD THIGH-DEEP IN the surf, holding a spear in his hand and staring into the foamy water swirling about his legs. The spear was shorter and lighter than the ones he and the others had used in bringing down the boar. This one was intended for fish.

Jin stood only a few yards away in what looked to Jeff to be identical circumstances, yet he had already speared three moderately large fish, while Jeff had yet to even see one.

Still, Jeff was enjoying himself. The sun was bright and warm, the water cool and refreshing, and the task required just enough thought to keep his mind off other matters. That's what he wanted more than anything these days—something that would make him stop thinking about Savannah, stop obsessing over the weird events at the cave. He tried to be pragmatic, telling himself that it had happened and now it was over. Let it go.

He couldn't let it go, though. He thought about it almost every waking minute.

That was why he was glad to be, at the moment anyway, thinking of little else than spotting and spearing a fish. Staring into the shallow surf was rather hypnotic and he entertained himself by humming a melancholy air he had often heard when he was growing up on the island of Arran.

> *I dreamt it last night*
> *That my dead love came in*
> *So softly she entered*
> *Her feet made no din*
> *She came close beside me*
> *And this she did say*
> *It will not be long, love, until*
> *Our weddin' day.*

In truth, that beautiful old Celtic song drifted through Jeff's mind almost daily. He had always loved it on its own terms but now it meant something more personal. His dead love had truly come in, and it was no dream.

A long time ago, a lifetime ago, he had lain beside Savannah under that scratchy blanket in his studio and she had talked of a love that could exist beyond death, beyond time. "Do you think such a thing truly exists?" she had asked.

No. I emphatically do not, he had said to himself. But

what he had said aloud to her was, "Well, of course I do. Of course I do."

And now he did.

There were over forty castaways stranded on the island by the crash of Oceanic Flight 815. And that meant that Jeff was asked nearly ninety times what had happened at the cave. Because Hurley and Charlie had regaled listeners with tales of their terrifying experience with the invisible monster on the boar hunt, Jeff found that he was able to be as cryptic as he liked about the cave and people seemed to be satisfied. "It was just one of those mysterious things that sometimes happen here," he would tell them. "It's entirely unexplainable."

He sometimes even described the shadowy creatures with their awful groaning whispers, and told in morbid detail about how the things slashed at him and Michael with what must have been razor-sharp fingernails.

"But what were they?" he would say. "I have no idea. I only know that I don't want to go anywhere near where that cave was anymore, and I'd suggest that you steer clear of that damned place as well."

In short, Jeff told the truth about it . . . to a point. He never mentioned Savannah or her child. And he never tried to explain what he began to feel was the real story, that the things were not island mysteries like the invisible thing at all, but personal mysteries, aimed at no one other than Jeff.

To some extent the experience brought Jeff out of his

shell. He got to know other castaways, worked with them, played golf or swam with them, and began to feel like a member of the community instead of the hermit he had been for so long.

But in another way, the puzzling occurrence at the cave made Jeff even more introspective. He thought about it every day. Since Michael remembered almost no details of the day and Locke saw nothing out of the ordinary, Jeff sometimes almost convinced himself that it was nothing more than a hallucination. If he could truly have made himself believe this, it would have meant a great deal more peace of mind for Jeff—as in the lyrics of the song, people dream of their "dead loves" all the time. And sometimes those dreams are so real that even when the dreamer wakes up it is difficult to shake the feeling that there has been an actual encounter, a meeting across the boundaries of death.

But Jeff knew that what he had gone through was no dream. Savannah had come to him. She had come to save his worthless life, as she had once predicted she would, but also to tell him something. And still, after nearly a month of daily concentration, of replaying the events ceaselessly in his memory, he had no idea what that something was.

There was a silvery movement near Jeff's feet. Instinctively, he jabbed the spear straight down into the water and felt it make contact. Pulling the spear out, Jeff was delighted—and more than a little surprised—to see a large fish wriggling on the point. He held it skyward and shouted happily, "Jin! Jin!"

Jin looked up and saw the fish. He grinned at Jeff and gave him a thumbs-up and then he went back to his own work. *Oh well,* Jeff said to himself, *that was pretty high praise from Jin.*

Jeff walked to shore and threw his fish into the shallow pool Jin had dug in the sand and filled with seawater. That would keep them fresh until time for dinner. Jeff noted with a certain degree of pride that his was the largest of the lot.

"Big fish in a small pond," Jeff said to his catch. "That's what I was in Lochheath. And look at both of us now."

"Talkin' to a fish, dude?" Hurley said, sauntering onto the beach.

Jeff laughed. "Nothing wrong with that," he said. "As long as the fish doesn't talk back."

"Dude," Hurley said. "After the stuff I've seen, it wouldn't surprise me one bit."

"Me, either," Jeff said.

"I talked to Jack a while ago," Hurley said. "He said if you want to move into the jungle, it's fine with him. There's plenty of room."

Jeff nodded. "Yeah," he said. "Good."

"I think he's glad you want to," Hurley said. "He thinks if we all stick together in one place we can protect ourselves better."

"True," Jeff said. "But that's not why I'm doing it."

"Then why?" Hurley said. "That little place you've got is pretty sweet, almost like a real hut."

Jeff thought for a moment and then said, "I just don't need it anymore. I haven't made anything or drawn anything ever since . . . well, in almost a month. I almost have the feeling that I was led to the studio for a reason, and now that reason is gone."

Hurley just looked puzzled. But then, he was often puzzled by the events on the island, so he had learned to have a certain degree of equanimity about it. He said, "Walt tells me you've been giving him drawing lessons."

Jeff grinned. "Yes, I have," he said. "He's really got a gift."

Jeff heard shouting from the surf and looked up to see Jin yelling something to him in a stern voice. Jeff couldn't understand the words, of course, but he knew that Jin was telling him to get back to work.

He said to Hurley, "Well, coffee break's over."

"Yeah," Hurley said. "Back on your head."

Jeff returned to his place in the water and gripped his spear, ready for another big catch. But though he stood there for another hour, he never even saw another fish. He smiled apologetically to Jin as Jin strung together the fish to take over to the cooking fire. Surrounding Jeff's single fish were nearly a dozen caught by Jin. *But mine,* thought Jeff, grasping for some way to salvage his pride, *is still bigger than any of his.*

Jeff walked down the beach until he came to the cove with the little waterfall that had served as a marker on his journey to the cave. There was no one else around, so he stripped off his clothes and dove into the clear, fresh water. It was bracingly cold, far colder than the seawater. He swam about for a few moments, enjoying feeling clean and refreshed. Then he stood under the waterfall and enjoyed the gentle pounding of the water as it massaged him.

The sun glinted off the water, making the pool sparkle like jewelry. The shimmering light turned each drop into a tiny prism, and beautiful, subtle rainbows seemed to sprout everywhere before exploding into pure color. Jeff had to squint when the reflections were at their brightest; the dancing rays created a glistening palette of shifting shapes.

Jeff floated around on his back for a while and then splashed noisily, feeling like a child. He remembered how much he used to enjoy going under the water and seeing how long he could hold his breath, and decided to give it a try now. Taking in a big gulp of air, he dropped beneath the surface. He swam to the bottom of the pool, which was clearly visible due to the brightness of the sunlight. It was a fascinating world of silence and tranquility and Jeff wished that there were a way he could stay there longer. But his lungs were beginning to burn and he knew it was time to resurface.

As he swam upward, he saw someone standing by the side of the pool. *Well, this might be embarrassing,* he thought. *I'm naked as the day I was born.*

When he broke the surface, he took a deep breath and wiped the water from his eyes. He turned in the direction of the figure by the pool and said, "I must warn you to look the other way if . . ."

The temperature of the water seemed to drop another ten degrees. Or Jeff might have started shivering for another reason.

Savannah was standing at the pool's edge.

Jeff was treading water and the sight of Savannah nearly made him drop back under. He scrambled out, not bothering to think about his clothes, and ran toward her.

"Savannah . . ." he cried.

But she was no longer there.

Jeff stood on the spot where he had seen her and looked around for any proof that what he had seen was real. He found nothing. After a moment he gathered up his clothes and dried himself with his shirt. He then dressed and began walking back to the studio.

I dreamt it last night
My dead love came in . . .

He stood at the narrow entrance that led into his natural house. Something made him hesitate to go in. As he had told Hurley, Jeff had determined that he was through with this place. He had only created dark and disturbing works here, and the clues those works left him had solved nothing, but led only to deeper and darker mysteries. There were no answers here. There were no answers anywhere. Tomorrow he would move into the caves with the others, and then his past life would be officially over.

Jeff ducked slightly to enter the studio. It was darker inside but numerous spaces in the branches and leaves that formed a kind of roof allowed in the sun in tiny points of light like, as Jeff often amusedly thought of it, a disco ball.

It took only a few seconds for his eyes to adjust to the dimness of the space and as soon as they did, he noticed it. There on the ground in the center of the studio lay a wooden disc onto which had been carved an intricate and strange design.

It was the talisman.

22

JEFF PICKED UP THE disc from the ground and turned it over and over in his fingers. The last time he had seen it was back in the cave, when Savannah retrieved it after Jeff had flung it to the floor. And now it was back.

And Savannah was back, too.

He felt her before he saw her. Turning slowly, both eager and fearful, Jeff looked to his left to find Savannah seated on the ground, cross-legged. It was exactly the way she used to sit when . . .

A chill went up Jeff's spine. *When she was alive.*

Jeff began to tremble. The first time he tried to speak, his voice sounded only in a hoarse squeak. He held the talisman out to her and tried again. "You brought this?" he said.

Savannah smiled a natural, friendly smile. "I returned

it," she said in the same strange language Jeff had first heard at the cave.

"Why?" Jeff said.

"It's yours."

Jeff stepped toward her. He said, "May I sit down?"

"Of course," Savannah said. "But you mustn't try to touch me. It isn't possible."

Jeff sat down before her and crossed his legs like her. He stared at her in wonder for a long time. She said nothing but simply smiled patiently. She looked solid, real . . . living.

Finally, Jeff said, "Are you a ghost?"

Savannah looked as if she were thinking of just the right words to say. "I am . . . myself."

Jeff tried again. "Is this a dream?"

"Life is but a dream," Savannah said. Then she laughed and added, "Row, row, row your boat."

"Well," Jeff said, feeling somehow more comfortable, "I've never been mocked from the Other Side."

Savannah laughed. "Not that you know of!" she said.

"Why are you here?" Jeff asked.

Savannah again looked thoughtful. She reminded Jeff of someone from a foreign country trying to translate her thoughts into an unfamiliar language. "I am here so . . ." she thought again. "I am here so that you will know."

"Know what?"

"What do you want to know?" Savannah asked.

Jeff threw his hands in the air and nearly shouted, "I want to know everything!"

"Typical Jeff," she said. "Wanting more than you can get."

Jeff shook his head. "All right, then," he said. "I want to know whatever you can tell me."

Savannah once more knitted her brow in thought. "This will not be easy to explain to you," she said at length. "I cannot really *tell* you anything. But I can make you *know*."

She stood up. "I can stay no longer."

Jeff sprang to his feet, his arms outstretched. "No . . . please . . ."

Savannah stepped back. "Remember—you cannot touch me."

Jeff dropped his arms and they hung dejectedly at his sides. "Don't go. I've missed you so much."

"I know," she said.

"It was the stupidest thing I ever did . . ." he said. Tears began to course down his cheeks.

"I know," she said.

Jeff said, weeping harder, "Do you hate me?"

Savannah smiled more brightly than ever. "I love you, Jeff. I will love you forever. I came to you, didn't I? Beyond death. Beyond time. No one makes that journey through hate."

"I love you," Jeff said. "You're the only woman I ever loved."

Savannah said, "I know that, too. Everything is all right." She began to fade from sight.

"No!" Jeff shouted. "Not yet! Tell me!" He gestured

around the studio to all of his grotesque artworks. "What are these?"

Her voice was faint and her face looked as if it were behind a cloud of steam. "Those are directions," she said. "From me to you. From you to me."

And then she was gone.

Jeff collapsed to the ground, his body wracked with sobs. He clutched the talisman tightly in his hands and wept for what seemed like hours. And then, just as suddenly, he stopped weeping and sat upright, a look of wonder on his face. He couldn't explain how or why, but now he *knew*. What Savannah had just said was true. She couldn't explain anything to him, but she could make it so that he would know. And he did.

"Those are directions," she had said. "From me to you. From you to me." Savannah had drawn the designs in her sketchbook without knowing why, and once he was on the island, Jeff began to draw them himself. He had thought they were simply abstracts, interesting yet meaningless; and after they started coming to him almost every day, he began to think that his artwork held some sort of sinister motive. He was compelled to carve the talisman after seeing Savannah in his dream showing it to him, and mistakenly thought that it was there to ward off the evil that he met that day at the cave.

But the talisman and the other designs were simply, as Savannah explained, directions—signposts that would allow him to find her and she him, even when they were living in different dimensions. Jeff had once told her that the designs looked like hieroglyphics from a civilization that never existed and Savannah had answered, "Don't be so sure." And now he knew that the language did exist, and had always existed. But it was a language understood only by two people, that would bring them together in their hour of greatest need.

And Jeff also realized that he knew, with a degree of relief, that Savannah had not committed suicide. When she appeared in his dream with slashed wrists, he had made the natural assumption and blamed himself for her despair. But now he could recall the awful sequence of events of her final day almost as if he had seen them himself.

Three days after Jeff had left her weeping hysterically among her half-packed luggage, Savannah woke up feeling ill. She rushed into the bathroom and vomited until there was nothing left in her stomach but bile. After three days in a row of similar bouts of nausea, she noticed that her period was late. After still three more days of weeping and worrying, she went to see her gynecologist, who examined her thoroughly and then congratulated her on the impending arrival of her first child.

Jeff had already left for Australia and Savannah didn't know what to do. He had made it clear enough that he wanted nothing more to do with her. If she came to him with the news that she was pregnant with his child, certainly he would think that she was trying to entrap him, tie him to her through a lifelong obligation. She couldn't face the possibility that he would react to the news with disgust, horror, or anger. But she also knew that it was wrong to bear his child without his knowledge.

Savannah expected Jeff to return to Lochheath in the early summer, just after her graduation. She determined that she would meet with him then. She would be very pregnant indeed by that point and she would try to explain as calmly and as rationally as possible that she expected nothing from him and that if he wanted to have a relationship with his child, Savannah would try to remain as unobtrusive as possible.

But it was then that Savannah heard someone at school saying that Jeff wasn't coming back. He was traveling straight from Sydney to Los Angeles. He might not come back to Scotland for a year or more. Maybe he would never come back. She went home to her apartment, unsure about what to do.

When she walked into her flat, she noticed her sketchbook lying open on the kitchen table. Savannah was puzzled—as a bitter memory of her time with Jeff, the sketchbook had been kept on a closet shelf for weeks. But now it was open to the pages that held some of the odd and unexplainable designs that she had drawn. One in particular caught her eye. When she drew it, it had seemed nothing more than a meaningless, if slightly unsettling, jumble of lines and curves. Now, the picture clearly contained the drawing of an airplane with the number 815 written on it.

Savannah was flabbergasted. She knew that she had drawn no such thing.

Several other faculty members and students had corresponded with Jeff while he was in Sydney, so it was little trouble to find out the name of his hotel. And when she called there to find that he had already checked out, she asked the name of the airline. The clerk had arranged for the cab and told her Jeff was flying on Oceanic.

Savannah rushed to her computer, logged on, and began searching for information about the flights leaving that day from Sydney to Los Angeles. There was only one.

Flight 815.

Panicking, Savannah rushed from her apartment, jumped into her car, and began speeding toward the local airport. She didn't know exactly what she was going to do once she got there, but she had the vague idea of flying to Los Angeles. To protect Jeff.

The traffic was infuriatingly slow on the road to the airport and Savannah kept her hand pressed to the car horn, all the while knowing that it would do nothing to speed things along. When she found herself trapped behind a slow-moving garbage lorry, Savannah impulsively veered her car onto the shoulder of the road to pass on the left side. The shoulder was narrower than she expected and her car plunged off the road into a gully. Instinctively, Savannah let go of the steering wheel and held her hands in front of her to shield herself from the impact. Both of her arms crashed through the windshield; the shattered glass cut wide gashes across the veins in her wrists.

Savannah gingerly drew her arms back inside, recognizing with ultimate irony that she probably would have remained uninjured if she had kept both hands on the *wheel. She stared in shocked bemusement as her blood pulsed out in thick, dark geysers. Looking to the side, she saw a cow in a pasture, watching her curiously. She was gazing into the cow's large eyes when everything went dark.*

Savannah had known that Jeff had to be protected from something and she had died trying to come to his aid. And now Jeff knew, as tears stung at his eyes, that even after death, she had recognized from wherever she was that at least one of the island's mysteries was going to bring him greater danger than ever. And so she came again, and rescued him at last.

The speckles of light from the sun began to disappear and the interior of the studio was almost totally dark before Jeff stirred. He felt like he had been asleep but knew that he hadn't been. And once again, he felt as if he had been dreaming. But he hadn't been—he knew that he had only been listening to what Savannah had been telling him.

23

BRILLIANT SHAFTS OF BLUE and gold streaked across the sky as the sun prepared to make its final plunge below the horizon. At one point in his life Jeff would have likened the gorgeous sight to a Maxfield Parrish painting. But now he took the beauty of the sunset on its own terms. As he emerged from the studio, his arms filled with island artwork, he paused for a few seconds to bask in the vibrant colors of sunset, and then moved on to the pile. All of the statues, sculptures, carvings, drawings—everything he had made since he arrived on the island—were now unceremoniously stacked down on the beach near the huge piece of fuselage, that somber monument to Flight 815.

Or perhaps "unceremoniously" was the wrong word.

Jeff had gathered up the pieces, carried them across the sand, and readied them for something that felt very much like a ritual. This would be his farewell to the darkness of the past, his embrace of a new and, he hoped, better life, a celebration of his conviction that the rest of that life would be spent right here on this island, with these people.

Jeff was comfortable, almost happy, with the idea. Returning to Scotland now had no appeal to him. Without Savannah it would seem only like a cold, hard place filled with bittersweet memories of all that he had lost through his own pride and stupidity. There was much here on the island that was mysterious, much that was frightening, and much that was dangerous. But, Jeff felt, couldn't that be said for nearly anywhere in the world? On this remote tropical isle, there was also beauty and at least the potential for tranquility. He would take the good with the bad and he would make the best of it.

Jeff saw Kate sitting and chatting with Sun. He called out to her and both women waved at him. Kate arose, said a few words to Sun, and then trotted over to Jeff.

"Hey there," she said. "Housecleaning?"

Jeff nodded. "Now that it's getting dark, I thought all this would make a lovely bonfire," he said. "Want to join me?"

Kate smiled. "It *is* getting a little chilly," she said. "Light 'er up!"

Jeff took the piece of paper on which he had drawn the disturbing portrait of the shadow creatures and crumpled it loosely into a ball. He pulled out the cigarette lighter he had borrowed from Sawyer, flicked it once, and then held the tiny flame to the paper. When it was lit, Jeff carefully placed the burning drawing into a hollow place he had prepared near the bottom of the pile. Soon, the dry wood, paper, and leaves were blazing brightly.

Now they're beautiful, Jeff thought. *All those terrible things . . .*

"Nice," Kate said.

Jeff nodded. "Yes. It's rather like a funeral pyre, isn't it?"

Kate laughed. "Well, pleased to meet you, Mr. Morbid."

Jeff laughed, too. "No, I meant it in a far more positive way. This is a funeral for a lot of bad stuff. Good riddance."

They watched the yellow and orange flames dance brightly for a few moments and then Kate said, "You've never told me the real story, you know."

"About the cave?" Jeff said. "Of course I did."

"Hey, don't lie to a liar," Kate said. "There was something else that happened that day. Something you wouldn't tell anybody about."

Jeff's face and eyes reflected the fire as he considered whether to tell Kate the whole story about Savannah. "Do you believe in ghosts?" he said after a moment.

Kate grinned and said, "No."

Jeff laughed again, harder this time. "Neither do I," he said. "But I believe in angels."

. . .

The next morning Jeff awoke in the studio once more. Now that all of his artwork was nothing more than a pile of ashes, the place seemed positively cheery again. Sure the caves might be safer, but Jeff decided that he liked it here and here he was going to stay.

But I know one thing that will spruce the place up, he thought.

He pulled a piece of paper from the suitcase where he had kept it for the past weeks. Unfolding it, he carefully smoothed out the creases. Then he placed the sheet of paper on the ground, propped up against the trunk of a thick bamboo tree. It was the superhero drawing that Walt gave him the day after the incident at the cave.

I won't be able to get any glass, but I can carve a nice frame. That would be a good project, Jeff thought.

Jeff sat for a moment looking at the drawing, smiling. Then he realized that for the first time in over a month, he had awakened inspired to create something. He fished in his suitcase for another piece of paper. There wasn't much left; he'd have to be very careful from here on out.

He propped the suitcase on his knees so that he could use it as a desk and then he took out one of his two surviving pens and began to draw.

This picture was not filled with the strange, unsettling shapes and imagery of his previous island work. It was a portrait of Savannah. Now there was no surrealistic setting, no homage to other artists or styles. This was a representation of her face drawn with as much detail as love could muster, an image of optimism, beauty, and tranquility. It was a portrait that Jeff hoped might help to free them both from the ugly mistakes of the past.

The last time Jeff saw Savannah alive she had been weeping in agony at the pain he had caused her. The last words she said to him then were, "You will never live a day of your life without thinking of me."

Jeff Hadley smiled and continued sketching. Savannah's prediction was true so far, and Jeff knew that it would be true for the rest of his life.

The must-have book for fans.

Includes a detailed episode guide, behind-the-scenes looks and back stories to help uncover the mysteries of *Lost*.

Lost Season 2 Wednesdays 9/8c abc